# HIEROGLYPHS

OF

# BLOOD AND BONE

D1736049

By
Michael Griffin

Trepidatio Publishing

TREPIDATIO
PUBLISHING

Trepidatio books may be ordered through booksellers or by contacting:

Trepidatio Publishing an imprint of JournalStone

www.trepidatio.com

The views expressed in this work are solely those of the authors and do not necessarily reflect the views of the publisher, and the publisher hereby disclaims any responsibility for them.

ISBN:      978-1-945373-52-7      (sc)
ISBN:      978-1-945373-53-4      (ebook)

JournalStone rev. date: February 24, 2017

Library of Congress Control Number:      2017930774

Printed in the United States of America
2nd Edition

Cover Art & Design:  99designs - Biserka
Images:  bigstockphoto - image-118413428

Edited by:      Aaron J. French

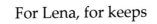

For Lena, for keeps

*Je me crois en enfer, donc j'y suis.*
(I believe I am in Hell, and so I am there.)

-Arthur Rimbaud,
*Une Saison en Enfer* (A Season in Hell)

# HIEROGLYPHS

## OF

# BLOOD AND BONE

# PART 1

# THE PSYCHOSIS

# OF

# HEARTBREAK

# Chapter 1

### Wild cries from another room

Since my divorce, I've been staying with Karl. He's constantly saying my real problem is that I'm too passive around women, and that's probably why Michelle ended things. Because this is Karl's place, I have to listen to him, at least pretend to appreciate the advice. But the two of us are so different, he's incapable of understanding me. Different backgrounds. Opposite temperaments.

I met Michelle in college, and after graduation she married me. That lasted twenty-one years. She's a beautiful woman, possessed of well-developed preferences and strong personal aesthetics. Off the top of her head, Michelle can list all the greatest poets, modern or classical, and the most notable films of Tarkovsky or Kubrick. She'll offer not only a ranked list, but fully reasoned explanations, an encyclopedia of references and connections, merits and demerits. If you want to know which Philip Glass or Steve Reich recordings to own, which to avoid, she'll tell you. Her expertise encompasses all art and culture, especially serious music and literature, but her deepest love is poetry.

Karl is dismissive when I tell him things like this. "So much bullshit," he says.

Karl never finished college, but because he's earning seventy thousand a year and he's only twenty-nine, he feels assured in his contempt for "all that snob shit." That's how Karl talks. Everything's simple.

"If this woman's so perfect for you, Tiger, how shitty was your game, to fuck that up?" he asks. "Shouldn't you be sharing her bed still, instead of mooching off this guy?"

How can I answer that?

I pay Karl five hundred a month for the second bedroom in his houseboat on the Oregon side of the Columbia River. My window looks across the river at Washington. His place is small, but it's convenient. Karl and I work at Constant Marine, a boat yard three miles down Marine Drive. That's a five-minute commute, compared to forty-five minutes from my house. I mean Michelle's house. She's the one who lives there now. I still think of it as mine, because I'm still paying the mortgage. That wasn't stipulated in the divorce settlement, but Michelle wants to wait for property values to rebound enough so she can sell the place. Then she'll pay me back.

Most evenings after work, Karl expects me to go out with him. He always chooses a spot, the kinds of places he insists single guys should want to go. "A fella's got to aim the right direction, if he's gonna get any," he says. What he means is encounters with women. I keep trying to explain my problem with this. A crowded bar is the kind of setting where I have no justification to approach someone. How exactly is meeting women this way supposed to work?

"Just get their digits." Karl shrugs. "Hit 'em up later. If you're too bawk-bawk-chickenshit to call and talk, that's what texting's for."

Then what? Karl's answers are never much help.

"Come the fuck on, Tiger." Lately Karl calls me Tiger. He thinks it's hilarious, this sporty young fella nickname, applied to someone like me. Karl says I've got a stick up my ass. I'm old. Too uptight.

He says, "Must keep a stiff upper lip, righty-o, old Tiger?"

He calls me "Lovey" in an accent like Thurston Howell III from *Gilligan's Island*. Karl's a TV Land addict whose knowledge of the shows I grew up with is better than my own.

He says, "It's not like you never hooked up before. Twenty years married, you must've hit that a time or two."

I don't have any response.

Karl shrugs. Always shrugging. "Important thing is, they want to hook up, you want to hook up. Why the shit not?"

He's better than me at arguing, even pointless, invented disagreements. Karl has endless energy for debate. If I do manage to score a point, he dismisses it with a funny-face shrug, or makes farting noises with his mouth. The thing is, I know he's really trying to help me. So I follow Karl to various places I don't exactly enjoy. Sports bars, chain restaurants, brewpubs. Mostly I feel like I've been dropped off in the wrong country, or the wrong decade. Maybe both. Not just disinterested for my own part, but certain of the scalding lack of interest younger women feel toward men like me, when they can have more confident guys like Karl. Not that he's as handsome as I am, or dresses as well, but Karl is two decades younger. More important than youth, he possesses that blithe self-confidence, an absolute smirking lack of give-a-shit women find appealing. At least, women we find in places like Jammer's.

Karl gets disgusted with me sitting back, sipping and watching. "Don't be such a fucking pussy, Felix Unger. That's what you are. Wait. Who's the one in *The Odd Couple,* the uptight sissy-bitch one?"

This time, I'm the one who shrugs.

"Why be such a chickenshit?" Karl fumes. "You got nothing to lose. I think your ex still got you pussy-bound."

That's another of Karl's frequently voiced theories, the only explanation he can possibly imagine as to why a hetero male, not yet completely over the hill, wouldn't aggressively pursue his next taste of the female unknown.

I'm not hung up on Michelle as a perfect ideal. I realize she has shortcomings, or at least aspects of temperament so contrary to my own as to render improbable our reconciliation. I'm aware of that reality. Bitterly aware.

Going to these places, Karl and I drive separate cars, in case he needs to leave without me. He never knows when he'll strike a gusher, to employ his preferred phrase. I sometimes mimic, joking with him. I play the Tiger. It feels awkward, even pretending.

When Karl does strike a gusher, he smirks on his way out the door, one hand raised like a sportsman in celebration. Rounding the bases or something. Maybe he thinks rubbing my nose in his success will inspire me. Really it's a relief. I'm not trying to play his game. This routine wears on me, these dismal settings, sitting on fake leather seats, being served beer and fried food on fake wood tables. Karl's teasing encouragement, his misguided efforts to coach me onward, not toward the next relationship, but something he considers more important. Rebound sex.

Sometimes I daydream about stopping, just refusing to play along. Remain Karl's roommate and coworker, but discontinue these boys' nights.

It never comes to that. Though Karl has always seemed to prefer a sequence of brief connections to an actual relationship, the unexpected occurs. Karl finds himself a girlfriend. She's someone unknown to me, apparently some contact dating back to before I moved in. I press for details, expecting him to offer some nugget of smirking misogyny like, *Remember the big-titty blond from Pinochle Bar?*

In fact, he merely shrugs, mutters something indistinct. "Pretty sure you don't know her."

Karl no longer wants to go trolling after work. I should be relieved. Have I mentioned he calls it trolling?

Evenings change so abruptly that I find myself fondly missing our sports bar evenings. I spend nights alone, looking around the little houseboat, listening to the river move, waiting for something. Karl occasionally brings the girlfriend around, but not so I can meet her. He only ever returns home after I've turned in.

Then finally one night, she's there. I know because I hear.

There's no avoiding the sound through the walls. A woman's repeated cries, shrill breaths and whines of animal pleasure. I feel envy, frustration. These noises aren't for me.

Some guys, alone after their divorce, might say they're happy for a roommate who brought a woman home. Those guys would be lying.

I know there's something wrong with me now, some change since things ended with Michelle. It might not be visible in my face. I feel a desperate, starving need, one I'm aware of constantly. This hunger emanates from me, a shrill, pathetic sound. Even when I sleep it won't relent. I have dreams of concentrated desire and need, as if feminine spirits, or at least Michelle's narrowed eyes, watch over me, mocking. This sense amplifies my loneliness and craving, my sense of being judged. Something eternally feminine, disembodied though it may be, hovers outside my window, attuned to pitiful vibrations issuing from my bruised and maddened brain. If I'm able to look quickly enough at the right angle, at the correct juncture between waking and sleep, I might glimpse one of these wavering spirits in the air.

I've passed beyond the limits of human want and craving. This aching oversensitivity attunes me to perception on unknown wavelengths. I overflow with lust, my imagination an over-amplified circuit, sizzling with possibility. Eventually this electricity has to either destroy me or attract what I require.

That sound beyond my door, I'm not trying to hear. Is there a difference between *not trying to* listen, and *trying not to*? I cover my head with a pillow, but that doesn't quiet my thoughts. My bedroom so dark, nothing visible. I'm alone. Where else can my attention go?

Hard, deep breaths, rising to extended cries.

What am I supposed to do with this primal, clenching response in my gut? Trembling alertness, and anxious physical arousal. I believe her cries convey a sense of who she must be, though in truth I know nothing. Remember what it was like being with Michelle? She was never so unrestrained. The sounds carry echoes of past life into this present moment. I'm alone, experiencing nothing physical at all. Just listening. Not that I'm putting myself in Karl's place. I'm not.

Full-throated yelling. A culmination.

How do I know this is real? This isn't the kind of fantasy I'd create. She sounds like she's in pain. Her guard is down, passion rendering her unreservedly wild.

This woman I've never met. Not that I want her for myself, this specific person. I know nothing about her, can't even visualize. I close my eyes, try to see Michelle's face, imagine these cries emitting from her. My imagination shifts, the face changes. It's no longer Michelle. By slow degrees, she transforms in every aspect. Completely new. More accepting, not judgmental. No questions. Nothing at all like Michelle, more her opposite. That's who I see.

Maybe I sleep. Sounds carry between rooms, merge into imagination or dreams. I feel a sense of having briefly possessed a woman of my own. Some strange, ideal person never met, body and face unseen. A stranger's indefinite shape. A voice defined by gasps and moans. Dreams don't require a name.

I jump alert, fully awake. Sudden sharp awareness of midnight solitude. I feel foolish, permitting myself to indulge such thoughts, but I'm alone here. Nobody else knows. It's just sad, imagining myself with my roommate's girl. Is that what I've been doing? Karl's the one with someone in his bed. Not me. It's humiliating, lying here frustrated, sweating through my sheets.

*Just stop.*

I must've dreamed some of it. Some of the sounds I remember are inhuman, wild animal wailing. A mournful, anguished cry of a lonely soul in the wilderness, awaiting solitary death. That's what my mind conjures. All this from the sound of some strange woman fucking my roommate.

In darkness, she's not the only one lacking identity. I'm the same. My thoughts carry no name, display no face, bear upon them no imprint of myself. Whose room is this? Not mine. The man I've been for twenty-five years is absent now. I'm some other person, in a room I don't own. Just a visitor borrowing a partial life.

# Chapter 2

### In the dark a faceless woman

In a bed, in a room. Where am I? The sheets are drenched, tangled around me, my sweat. Everything dark, no moon beyond the window. Water sounds. I'm not home, but where? My mind rushes in animal fear. Unreal memories. A woman shrieking, gasping for breath, almost howling as if tortured. Like someone trying to make as much noise as possible.

The murmur of the Columbia River flowing. Remember. I'm renting a room from Karl. The alarm clock's glow remains hidden until I move the pillow.

3:33.

Now it's quiet. Maybe I'll drift off. I need some sleep. Always so tired lately, fatigue a constant ache.

In the trees, all dark, no moonlight. Underfoot, a cushion of dry pine needles. Sightless eyes, no help at all. Long howls, voice intermingling with wind blowing through woods. I step forward, hesitant, hands groping before me. Fingertips scrape something rough. A tree trunk. Warm air shifts, reverses. No more wind. Everything stops.

This room. I'm in bed. No trees. Still that sound.

I get up, open my door, peer into the hall. Not sure what I'm looking for. Curiosity drives me, or frustration.

A short hall connects our rooms, Karl's nearest the dockside front of the houseboat, mine toward the back. In the hall between us, a shared bathroom. I open my door without turning on the light, in case Karl's bedroom door is open. She was so loud, I wonder if they left their door open on purpose, maybe Karl's idea of a joke.

*Make sure old Tiger hears you.*

The black hallway, so still. My own breathing, and the floor creaks. I can hear, or least feel, the river swirling not far beneath my feet.

How long ago did she stop? Maybe just now. Maybe she heard my door open.

I'm not trying to see, don't want to impose myself. So what am I after? I crack open the bathroom door, flick on the switch. Indirect light reaches the hall.

Karl's door is open, the bedroom dark beyond the verge.

I'm listening, motionless. Can I hear breathing, other than my own? I step nearer Karl's open door.

Not my room, not my place. "Karl?" I whisper.

No answer. My eyes adjust, dilated pupils straining to make out shapes.

"Sorry," I say. "Thought I heard something."

The minimal spray of light ends just inside the doorway. The room is a black void. My eyes extend, try to reach, find something more.

There's someone seated on the edge of the bed. Bare legs smooth, hairless. Feet on the ground, toenails painted. A woman. Impossible to discern more.

Her voice out of the dark. "I'm the only one here now."

I freeze, feeling caught. Straining to see. No color, no features. Just an outline, a blurred photograph of a female nude. Feet together. Ankles, calves, knees, thighs. Can I make out a torso? Breasts, very white. Not sure how much I see, how much is imagination. A mystery.

"Where's Karl?" I ask.

"He'll be back," she whispers.

This seems like no answer, but I'm at least half asleep, too disoriented to manage any reply. My heart strains in my chest. I feel too self-conscious standing here, swaying back and forth on the verge of the doorway to my absent roommate's room, talking to some naked stranger. Need for sleep overtakes me, a sudden urgency. Fatigue refuses to be ignored. I can think of no more words, no reason to be here. I want to apologize, but instead back up, snap off the bathroom light.

The hallway goes dark, and there's nothing at all beyond that open door. Then I'm in bed, blinking against the thick, oppressive night, wondering whether I ever really got out of bed at all. Maybe I've been here the whole time, imagining.

I feel certain I've intruded. She has more right to be here in Karl's place than I do. She's in Karl's bed. I still want to know where he's gone, but can't ask again. I don't know what I was looking for. Anyway, it's so dark, she probably has no idea what I could see. Maybe she thinks she's invisible. Maybe she is. Sometimes eyes offer what we expect to see, especially after too much imagining.

Maybe I'll be able to sleep now, finally sleep. Mind relieved in blankness. Fatigue and arousal, competing sicknesses in my gut. But so often I've gone to bed, convinced I'm tired enough, then ended up stuck, mind racing, wondering where I went wrong.

For six months after I left Michelle, I never considered the next woman, where I might meet her, whether she'd be a drunken hookup facilitated by Karl, a rebound girlfriend, a prostitute, a second wife. Living in Karl's place, always swaying on the water of the Columbia, such an uncertain and foundationless approach to my future seemed plausible. Not starting over new, but waiting for my old life to recommence. How does a man, satisfied with stable work and contented marriage, transform so quickly into a traumatized victim of divorce? I watch too much standup comedy on cable, drink too much cheap whisky, and sleep nowhere near enough. When I was married, I took care of myself. Not anymore.

Somehow, things have to change. I've never been a bachelor, don't know how to perform that role. Michelle is no longer an option, no matter how many times I envision scenarios. I need something tangible. It's time.

At the moment I reach this decision, something within me relaxes, a trembling muscle finally unclenching after months of overwrought tension. I feel myself give in to the inevitability of change.

# Chapter 3

## Two men prepare to go fishing unencumbered

I'm up early, making sandwiches. Last week, Karl and I made plans for this morning, but everything might be out the window if the girlfriend is still around. The door to Karl's room is closed, and my curiosity is like an itch. I want to get a look at her in daylight.

There are sounds of movement just as I'm finishing up, stirring and footsteps. Karl's door opens, heard rather than seen, around two corners from the kitchen. I wait, but nobody emerges far enough for me to see. The bathroom door clicks shut, shower spray commences. No talking, just the usual commotion Karl makes getting ready each morning. One thing I grudgingly admire about Karl is his minimalist routine. Boot camp hair, beard trimmed weekly with electric clippers. He requires nothing but soap, deodorant, toothbrush and towel.

I move toward my bedroom, hoping to steal a glance down the hall. Karl's door remains open, but the room is empty. Unless she's in the shower with him, she must have already departed. I never heard her go. Though I don't remember getting any sleep, I must have drifted off. Maybe when I found her there, sitting on the edge of Karl's bed, she was getting ready to leave. That doesn't explain where Karl was.

The shower shuts off. I return to the kitchen, not wanting to be obvious. I listen for voices, the kind of interaction I'd expect between two crowded into our tiny bathroom, but all I hear is Karl stomping around. The sink runs briefly, then the door opens. Karl rounds into the kitchen, wearing gray boxer briefs and a white t-shirt, carrying his blue uniform shirt. "You almost ready, Tiger? Can't be late. We've both been ass-chewed one too many times."

I set the knife and cutting board in the sink, trying to guess whether he's kidding.

"Move it, get going," Karl says. "Two minutes." Not joking, apparently.

"Karl, you said we're going fishing."

"No, that's Saturday." His face shows such theatrical confusion, I wonder if it's a put-on. "Oh, fuck me running, today's Saturday. Well, that's cool. Fishing beats working."

"You're probably a little foggy. I'm guessing you didn't get much sleep either."

"Check this out." Karl lifts his t-shirt to reveal his right flank, a series of red inflamed scratches above the hip.

"I heard your yelling last night," I admit. "I mean, hers."

"Last night?" He looks at me crooked, seemingly mystified. "Just me here, by my lonesome. Turned in early." Karl twists, trying to examine around the side of his torso. "Jehoshaphat, Tiger, check out these marks. I'm all tore up."

"Sure." I laugh. "You were alone. You clawed yourself to pieces."

He looks like he really doesn't get it, but I'm not sure whether to take him seriously. Karl's constantly trying to get a rise out of me, always dropping some embarrassing goof, waiting to see if I'll fall for it. "Fuck, it's all raw." He traces a finger down the reddest wound. "Jesus."

I venture a high-throated, feminine whine, breath in and out fast. "Ohhh, owww, ohhh."

Karl doesn't seem to get it. Just looks at me like I'm nuts.

"You're saying you were alone here?" I confirm. "Last night?"

He nods, pulls down his t-shirt and throws the uniform shirt over the back of the couch, which forms a boundary wall between kitchen and living room.

"Karl, seriously, she was here. I got up to go to the bathroom, and your door was open. I couldn't help seeing her sitting there on the edge of your bed."

"Saw who?"

"I don't know her name. You never introduced us."

He shakes his head.

"A woman," I continue. "Your girlfriend. Who else would it be?"

Karl breaks up laughing, shaking his head. "So where was I during all this?"

"How should I know? I asked her, 'Where's Karl?' She just said, 'He'll be back.'"

"I never left, Tiger. My girl, she wasn't around last night."

"What's her name? Tell me what she looks like."

"She's out of town. And I definitely never left."

"So how'd you get all scraped up? You get a little too passionate with the self-love?" I made the sound again, a tense wail so high and piercing it pained my throat to make it. "Whining and crying, howling all alone like that?"

"Stop that shit, Tiger. Hurts my ears. She's out of town, visiting family. These sex fantasies of yours, Jehoshaphat, Tiger. Sexual frustration will drive a man fucking unbalanced. See, here's the reason you need to go fishing. You know why so many old guys love to fish? Distraction from that traffic jam taking place in your nut sack."

I'll grant Karl one thing, he knows how to shut me up.

"Her name's Sadie." Karl rubs his side. "I'll see her tonight. Wonder what she's going to say about these scratches?"

"When she comes over, I want to ask her if she was here. See what she says, without any coaching from you."

"Sure, bro. I'm telling you, Tiger, hormone seepage is getting into your bloodstream. Your brain's poisoned by the DSB."

"Sure, bro." I want to change the subject. "I made sandwiches, plus Coke for you, iced coffee for me. It's all in the ice chest. You say I need fishing. Let's go."

"Said it's a substitute, didn't say it's a good substitute." He looks at me, mock serious, puts one hand on his hip, juts it sideways like a supermodel. "Tiger. Seriously, it's time."

"I get it, I know. Really. I'm over Michelle."

"No."

"It's a process. I'm getting out into the world."

"Bullshit. You're hanging around here all by yourself, like a pussy."

"I promise you. I'm not holding out for Michelle. Seriously."

"Michelle, that's her name?" He glares, pops his knuckles, like he's inspired to do violence.

"You know her name." I pick up the ice chest. "Let's go."

"It's time, that's all I'm saying. Maybe Sadie's got a friend. You interested?"

This catches my attention. I stand frozen, imagining some unknown woman, her face. It's just an idea.

"You are interested, I can tell. You horn dog. Okay, I'll do some digging, but if Sadie does have a friend, you can't be a pussy. You got to assert yourself a little. At least pretend you own a pair."

Maybe. The possibility gets me thinking. "I had weird dreams. Maybe that's what it was."

"I bet you have weird dreams." He makes a face, and goes back for weekend clothes.

A few minutes later, we're driving.

# Chapter 4

## Private land on the Kalama River

Karl parks just outside a yellow gate on the shoulder of River Road. A long driveway beyond the gate winds through pines and Douglas firs.

"You sure this is okay?" I grab the ice chest from the back seat.

Karl slams the trunk. Carrying fishing gear in both hands, he ducks under the gate. "Sure. I've been fishing this river since I was a little peckerhead."

"You're still one." It's a small thing, but joking with Karl on his level pleases me. I crouch and slip past the barrier.

I may have to revise my assessment of Karl. He's always played the carefree lecher, and carried his perfect lack of give-a-shit like a shield against the world. But now he has a stable girlfriend, and a job that compensates him well, even if it requires harder labor than I'd care to do. He persists in trying to push me along, nudge me through my difficult time. He doesn't understand me half as well as he believes, but he's trying to boost me, to prop me up as much as he's able. Even when he's driving me crazy, I appreciate his intentions. Even something like today's fishing trip, it's Karl's idea of something I may not realize I need.

Karl leads the way up the gravel driveway. "Lots of people fish the Kalama, but this block of land is private. The man who owns all this, our guy Cayson, he's this kingpin developer type in Northwest Portland. Once my pop helped Cayson with zoning, some warehouse deal in the Pearl, this is before the Pearl went all hot shit condos. So Cayson said we could use his property any time."

For weeks Karl's been trying to get me out here, first with vague suggestions about fishing, then challenging my expressed desire to try new things. When he started things up with the new girlfriend, I thought this might be forgotten, but he didn't let it drop. He kept mentioning this beautiful, quiet stretch of river twenty-some miles north into Washington, particularly these spots within canyon walls where you scramble down to find clear pools where a hundred steelhead are holding, resting out of the sun, willing to take a fly if you float it right through their midst. Karl has heard my counter-arguments, that fishing is dull and smelly, a poor exchange of time and effort for food. He's smart enough to recast it as an adventure of natural discovery, delving into untouched creases where ancient river cuts through rock, and primordial creatures wait hovering in transparent water, alien and otherworldly. Never using these exact words, of course. Most of the things I told him I dislike about the idea of fishing don't apply here. No elbowing throngs of fisherman swarming both banks. More like a private nature preserve.

A quarter mile up the gravel, just as a sizable gray house comes into view further along the driveway, we cut off to the right, toward the direction of the river.

"Looks like quite a place," I say.

"Cayson don't actually live here," Karl says. "It's pretty much a rich man's fishing hut. You could say Cayson owes my pop for everything he's got."

"I thought your dad was dead?" I say, and immediately wish I hadn't.

"He is dead, dumbshit." Karl glances sideways, only irritated for a moment. "That don't mean somebody like Cayson stops owing him."

As this offshoot trail curves nearer the river, I can hear the churn of water. To me, it's the sound of frustrated sleep. This sound is different, not a slower movement of a broad corpus of water, but a narrower and more varied churning over rocks.

"Here." Karl pushes through overgrown brush and vines at the top of the ridge.

The downslope is less drastic than I expect, after his talk of deep, hidden canyons. Dry soil gives way to a bank of river-smooth rocks, not far below.

"This isn't the place I mentioned, but we'll start here. It's easier." Karl begins laying out poles and assorted gear, dividing it in half. "This side's yours."

"Thanks."

I'm not sure how to proceed, so Karl does everything first, tying flies to leads, then leads to lines. I watch everything, and try to duplicate what he's doing. Casting seems tricky at first. I make mistakes, and Karl demonstrates what I'm doing wrong. He's unusually patient, almost serious. He describes aspects of the river, formations of rock and current, resulting in different kinds of water, each with a distinct name. Chutes, riffles, pools. We don't catch any fish, but Karl seems unconcerned, as if this isn't the point. He focuses on casting, watching the drift, reeling in. The repetition is quiet and rhythmic, almost meditative. The goal appears to be simple presence, a pleasingly mindless following of pattern, and watching the drift. Down near the water, the flow gives me a different sensation from that distracting flow beneath me every night on the Columbia. After so many sleepless nights, I'd love to think of the water in a different way.

One thing I love, an aspect unexpected, is how the line goes from well behind me, well out of view, to far ahead, with an almost effortless gesture.

It occurs to me I've been in a broken emotional state, all these months. I believed I was seeing clearly, but now I recognize I've been looking through some kind of heavy, obscuring veil. From the clarity of this moment, my recent mental state appears fragmented and dysfunctional. I wonder if I'll remember this insight when I return home, or just fall back into delusional misperception?

Upstream, Karl casts, watches the fly at the end of his line drifting down. He appears perfectly at peace, unaware of my presence.

If things within me have been tangled, I now feel a sense of opening up, at least a hint of the possibility that frayed ends may eventually be sorted. I'm not sure whether it's this place, or what we're doing here. I've never been interested in the outdoor life, always imagined it a realm of the physical. Maybe I'll grow into my physical side, or at least become more comfortable with the fact that it exists, it's part of me. Trees, sky, river. It's all so invigorating, like a chest full of cool air supercharged with oxygen.

"That pole and bag of gear," Karl says. "That's yours to keep. I've got too much stuff. Maybe you'll fish again."

"Thanks." I consider whether or not to smart-ass him back. "Just what the doctor ordered. Good, manly activity."

Karl doesn't rise to the bait, but remains serious. "What do you think it is, being a man?"

I regret opening the subject. "It's not... that I don't intend to move on. It's just that it was a long time, Michelle and me."

"Weren't you married forty years or something?"

"Fuck off. Twenty." There's something satisfying in replying to Karl in kind, coarse and direct.

"So, you know how to talk to a woman, how to live around a woman. How to fuck, even. Probably not very well, I'm guessing. Least you can find a hole once in a while."

"Karl." I don't feel like pursuing this direction, but maybe that's why I'm always stuck. I stubbornly resist any honest scrutiny of what's bothering me, what's holding me up. I'm great at analyzing others. "I only know Michelle. Not women in general. Only one."

"Sorry, Tiger, there's no difference. Ain't like your wife's a delicate gentlelady, and the kind of girls I meet are some kind of wild animals. Thinking like that's probably what got you divorced."

"Michelle..." I begin, trail off. "Michelle's difficult."

"Don't take this bad, Tiger, but your ex is a cunt."

I can't help being shocked, and even feel myself reflexively begin to defend Michelle. I realize these rationalizations are feeble and meaningless even before I speak them. "I get your point, it's just, that word is—"

"Use a different word, then. But this idea your ex is perfect, well, that's mistaken. She treated you like shit, and got you believing you deserve it. You should get something better, it's that simple."

I'm thrown off by Karl psychoanalyzing me, summarizing and explaining me.

"I say you need to demystify women," he continues. "Have an experience or two with some woman you don't love. Just be with her, see her for whatever she is, good and bad. Shit, women are mostly like men. Sure, they're built with different parts, and the hormones are different. But they're just another sex, not some higher form of life."

I want to go along, even agree with some of the things he's saying, but there's so much he doesn't understand. "I'm not someone who's just dived into life before. I've had my books, my wife. Now all that's left is my job, which you know I don't love. So what next? I have to think it all through. I'm not a man of action."

"No kidding," Karl says. "Your name's Guy, but you're the least guy-ish dude I know."

This makes me angry, Karl presuming he knows so much more about women that he can lecture me about Michelle. But I'm even angrier at myself, because I know he's at least partly right, that he's cut through all my denial and rationalization, gotten right to the core of truths I've avoided facing. Envy and jealousy start to rise in me. Why can't it be easier for me, like it is for Karl?

No. This isn't his fault. These feelings, my desperate fear, hatred of my own weakness. These are all mine.

I've stopped reeling and casting. My line is played out, far downstream.

"Come on." Karl reels in. "We'll fish those pools downriver now. That's the payoff. A hundred fat steelhead resting there, hiding from the sun."

I reel in too. We climb back toward Cayson's fields and parallel the river, which keeps dropping away below the level of the upper bank. This thin trail is all that exists between endless tall evergreens to our left, and the deepening river valley to our right. We walk without speaking.

After half a mile, Karl stops. "Careful here." He pushes through a gap in the overgrowth at the top of the bank. A rocky path drops steeply, at least thirty feet to the river. I scramble down, grasping roots and branches on my way.

"See?" Karl points.

In water clear as glass, a cluster of steelhead hover like silent hummingbirds levitating in air.

"Do it just like before," Karl says. "But here, there are more, and you can see 'em."

Without speaking, we cast into this otherworldly place. Karl stands upstream from me and works further out. I watch my line drift over the holding fish, casting a sharp shadow on the bottom of the pool. Time stands motionless. I breathe and cast, watch the slow movement, and repeat. No gravity, no time. As if we've disappeared from where we—

"Fish on!" Karl shouts.

I snap out of my reverie. "You've got one?"

"You, dummy."

Only then, I'm aware of commotion in the water. Frenzied tugging on my line.

"Pull back, not too hard." Karl feeds instructions, urgent but patient. "Reel in, but slow. Baby it."

I take in a little line, follow as the fish pulls left, then swerves back to my right. When the tension lets up, I reel in a few feet of line. This pattern repeats. The steelhead's struggle is straightforward, intuitively understood. All the rest of the fish have left the pool, scattered up or downstream. They no longer matter. There's only one fish, the one at the end of my line. The smell of the struggle is powerful, not a smell of fish, but disrupted water, my adrenaline and sweat, the dust stirred up by my feet, and spores of sunbaked ferns and the green vitality of vine leaves along the bank.

"Almost there," Karl shouts.

Soon I've got him near the bank, exhausted in the shallows, spinning feebly. His back is green-brown with black spots. He swoons over on his side, revealing a brilliant silver flank and white underbelly.

"You want to take this one." Karl rushes a few steps up the bank behind me, then hurries back to my side. "Here." He scoops the net under the fish, then offers me a little hardwood bat with lead weights in the end.

I shake my head. "I want to feel the fish." I kneel in the shallows. "I mean I want to hold onto it with my hands."

"You sure?"

I ignore the bat and lean into the water, grasp the fish near the tail and behind the head. It's heavy, cold. I'm not sure what I want, how to decide. Without letting go, I manage to slip the hook from the steelhead's mouth. Then I let it drop, and it jerks sideways, out of my grasp, and flops into the water. My fish swims away, into the center of the vacant pool.

"What..." Karl sputters. "That's what you meant to do?"

I straighten, back and shoulders aching, wondering what happened. The fish was caught, and now it's gone. Did I decide to let it go, when I could have easily taken it? When I saw it up close in Karl's net, when I thought about swinging the bat, killing the fish seemed like something I didn't want to do. The shift wasn't a conscious one. I came here today believing I wanted to take a fish, if I caught one. But when I had the chance, I hesitated. It got away.

"Well, anyway," Karl says. "I've got to get home early before Sadie comes back. Let's pack it in."

We reel in, separate and stow everything, climb up and out. On our way through Cayson's property, heading back toward the car, I feel serene, disconnected from my life. Any disappointment at losing the fish seems beside the point. Concerns about work, or Michelle. All worries are distant.

To my right, in the center of an open field of grass surrounded by receding evergreens, stands a little house or cabin. It's a broad A-frame, wider than its height. The place seems familiar, like something recognized from a photograph seen long ago. I wonder if it's still called an A-frame, when it's so wide like that. I turn to ask Karl, but he's gotten way ahead, still walking fast while I've slowed. He doesn't seem to notice what I've seen.

I hurry to catch up, and just as I'm about to pass out of the open field and reenter the forest, I glance back. The house is just a peaked box, a simple shape without windows or doors, no driveway or path connecting it to the world outside. It's completely isolated here, nestled between forest and river.

Then I'm startled to realize there's a woman outside, attaching something to the front of the house. I can't see her clearly, get no sense of her face. Dark hair, and she's barefoot, wearing some simple, colorless garment that blends into the wood. I wonder, was she there the whole time we walked by? Did she watch us pass, and say nothing? It's strange that I didn't see her until we were almost gone.

I run into the trees, trying to keep up. Karl seems in a hurry.

"Did you see that?" I ask Karl. "The little A-frame?"

Karl says nothing, just keeps walking.

I consider omitting mention of the woman, but I tell him what I saw. As I'm telling it, I realize I'm adding a detail or two I'm not completely certain I actually saw with my eyes.

"There wasn't any little house," Karl says, as if I'm being ridiculous. "And I sure as shit would've noticed some babe standing barefoot in the middle of a field there."

I don't argue. I know what I saw, and in fact become more certain the more I think of it. In the back of my mind, I know I'll revisit the memory later, try to see it more clearly, and make sense of it. It occurs to me, this is what I do, what I've always done. I walk away from experiences and encounters, leave them behind, figuring I'll make sense of them later, from a distance. As if imagination or memory is better than the real thing.

# Chapter 5

## What Michelle says and what she wants

My cell phone rings. Nobody ever calls except Karl or work or Michelle. It's late, so work's closed. Karl is crashed in his room, tired after fishing, apparently not going to meet his girl after all. I'm exhausted too, but can't sleep. I can't help it. I find myself hoping it's Michelle calling. She always calls after midnight.

I snatch up the phone. On the display, Michelle's name and number beneath her picture. I'm surprised at the irritation this photo inspires. Every anniversary, she insisted on paying for studio photos, both of us individually and as a couple. This was her last portrait before we split. Not a smile, but an emotionless show of too-white teeth.

My thumb hesitates only an instant over the green button. "Hello."

"It's me," Michelle says. "I hope you're not asleep?"

"No." What comes to mind is a series of possible responses, questions I might ask, lines of inquiry all quickly rejected. I can't guess which approach might work. Michelle is always a moving target.

Without further preamble, she launches into discussing aspects of her job, new coworkers, her boss. Then the house and something one neighbor said about another neighbor and the brick place down on the corner just sold. Other things, something about books. I find myself counting books on my shelf. Why? I've been anxious for Michelle to call, and now I can't be bothered to listen?

"Seventeen," I say to myself.

She keeps going, another sentence or two about whatever it was, then backtracks. "Seventeen what?"

"Books. That's my whole book collection. Seventeen books."

"No, Guy. You've got thousands of books."

"Not any more. You kept most of them."

"No. Well, any books I kept, it's because I liked them so much, I probably thought they were my own. You should consider it flattering to your taste if I respected one of your books so much. Actually it seems like the highest praise I can give."

I refuse to let myself consider whether or not I should be flattered. Still there's some tiny aspect in the back of my mind that feels pleased at her telling me she approves of something, anything about me. Wondering what that signifies. "So, you, Michelle. How are you?"

She sighs. "I wish we could see each other, Guy. Really, just talk. I miss that, talking. I do."

I have no responses for the moment. This is the worst, when she suggests the possibility of seeing each other, only to snatch it away if I seem interested. But I can't help wondering, what if this is the time? "If you really want to, we can. Have a drink. Something."

Her voice deepens, sounds throaty. "I'm not suggesting some liaison, Guy. I merely said I miss certain things. I'm being honest, like I hope you're honest with me. I miss certain things."

"I don't mean trying to restart our relationship. Sometimes people just meet and talk. You're the one who said it. I'm not trying to... Never mind. You brought it up."

"What, you never think about me anymore? You never miss conversations, after all we shared?"

"Of course. But if I call you up and say, let's have lunch, let's chat, you say, now Guy, don't get the wrong idea." This makes me hate myself, saying these things. I should hang up. I should never have answered. My hands are trembling.

"You sound angry," she says. "I'm just checking in. Saying hi."

"I'm not angry."

"I know you very well. I do know you very well, still." Her voice, a strained whisper. "And that's how you sound. Angry."

"I guess the thing I get frustrated about, Michelle, is you seem to enjoy toying with me."

"When you insert my name into the middle of a sentence it always means—"

"You insist that I should never call you, but when you call me, you expect me to be receptive."

"I don't expect anything."

"You do. You expect me to be glad to talk to you, not merely willing to talk, but actually happy to hear from you. Conversely, you expect me to never ask anything of you. You say you're sad we can't sit around and talk about, what was it, the stories of Raymond Carver, and was Tess Gallagher his equal as a poet. If I suggest we actually could talk about that, you say I'm trying to corner you, or rekindle—"

"That's not—"

"What am I supposed to say? If I miss that too, if I say I wish we could talk about things like that, you say, I'm not trying to get us back together, Guy. What if I say, who fucking cares what you miss? We're divorced, and it was your idea, and you're living in our house while I live in this shitty houseboat." I immediately regret this criticism of Karl's place, but don't want to halt my momentum. "I'm so sorry you miss our conversations, but you told me to leave. I have conversations with my roommate now, about things like fishing, and drinking, and scoring pussy. I have conversations at work about the owner's muscle cars, about Ducks football, and about the lottery tickets everybody buys. None of the conversations are about Raymond Carver or Tess Gallagher. There's nobody in my life who wants to discuss John Coltrane or Astrud Gilberto or David Lynch or Jackson Pollock. Those loftier avenues of discussion are simply not available to me, anywhere, ever."

"You need to get some friends, Guy. Maybe you need to date."

"Sure I do."

"I'm serious. I'm not calling you trying to rekindle—"

"I know. Not trying to rekindle. You keep saying."

"God, why are you making me out to be this insane bitch? I just called, mentioned something used to be nice. Something pleasant we shared. And you're angry."

"Yeah. I guess I am."

"Why are you angry? Ask yourself that. Can you not accept that we're no longer a couple, Guy? Our marriage is over. Still, we might talk. And if things went a certain way, who knows?"

I consider asking what that means, if things went a certain way. I can already hear the answer, so I ignore that impulse. "I'm not angry our marriage is over. Or if I am, I don't blame you for that."

"Then what?"

"I'm angry because you either want to be with me, or not. If not, why do you so often call and hint that you might? How am I supposed to—"

"I don't."

"You call, always after midnight, after a bottle of Pinot. Sometimes by the end, you're crying. Usually you are. You act like we're prevented from being together by outside forces. A tragic romance, doomed by circumstance. But nobody's keeping us apart. You didn't want me in the house, so I left. You wanted our marriage over, so we divorced. But calling up, pretending you wish you could be with me, if only, that's just an act of…"

"What?" Her voice rises an octave into shrillness.

"It's a fucking tease, Michelle. Game playing. Manipulation."

"Wow, damn. It sure does sound like you hate me, Guy. Do you actually hate me? I'm so sorry I called for a chat with my ex-husband, someone I loved and shared life with for a quarter century. More than half our lives. I'm sorry I mentioned a pleasant recollection."

"If you don't want this, fine. Just stop pretending, like we'd both rush back together if we could, but can't, like the plot of some romantic movie. You say I need to move on, but you're the one. We're divorced. You threw me out. I've got my room in the houseboat, I've got Karl, I've got my job. This seedling of hope is all I've got, this life I'm trying to rebuild out of not very much. Other than that, I've got nothing."

"Poor Guy. His fucking bitch ex-wife ruined his life. Isn't she horrible?"

"Michelle, please. Stop trying to keep your bridge to me open. You burned it. I finally see what you're doing."

"You're really so angry. You're furious. You keep saying you're not, and I could sense it. But just, wow."

"Fine. You've played this game over and over. Otherwise, why call me after midnight, and whisper in a soft, sweet voice about our beautiful, pleasant memories? Why say, oh, wouldn't it be lovely if we could get together and chat like before? I mean, if you wanted to, we could. We could have a normal talk. Not this. We could say, set aside worrying about the past, just eat a meal and drink a cocktail and talk about movies and books like we used to do. Two people sharing ideas. That's what I miss."

"See, we're on the same page, Guy." Her voice is soft again. "That's what I miss. It doesn't have to be some harsh conflict. You don't have to be angry."

She's gone full circle, as if she hasn't heard any of the things I've said. I'm frustrated, angry she won't listen, and worse, angry at myself for indulging this head game. I always know this is going to happen, and every time I try to speak up for myself, she manages to—

Then Michelle says the words. "You should know I'm getting married."

"Married?" My head thuds, a pulse heavy in my ears. "I didn't even know you started dating anybody."

Briefly I think, *she's going to marry the guy who tried to rape her Freshman year, just before we started dating. She'll go back in time and somehow find him, do the most fucked-up thing she could imagine, because she's trying to drive me insane.*

No, that's wrong. Stop.

"I told you about him," she says.

"You said you went on a date with that coworker who turned out to have a cocaine problem. But you didn't—"

"That's him. The drug thing, that was a misunderstanding. Probably I overstated it."

This time, maybe for the first time, I'm the one who hangs up.

# Chapter 6

## The sickness of living the wrong man's life

The more I grasp at sleep, the more remote it seems. I lie staring up into the dark, mentally listing all the things I want to change. I should approach life more like Karl. Everything's easy for him. Clearly my own approach isn't working.

After Michelle's call, I've been trying to concentrate on feeling proud of myself for standing up to her. Regret aches in my chest, connected to all the things it's too late to change. Not just Michelle remarrying so soon. I can't change myself in the ways I want. In fact I perceive myself changing in unwanted, physical ways. Since I've been living with Karl, I'm sweating more, my skin seems more oily. By the end of the day I smell myself, rank in a musky, typically masculine way, no matter what deodorant or cologne I wear. Hair grows from my nostrils and ears, places I don't remember seeing hair before. It's as if Karl's excess testosterone is overflowing into me. Or maybe that side of myself is only now waking up, since I'm free of Michelle. We met so young, and though I've always considered Michelle a civilizing influence, the truth is she probably shifted me toward being more feminine in my outlook. I don't think that works for me any longer.

So I'm trying on Karl's suggestions, seeing if I can be more casual, even though it's the opposite of my nature.

I realize there's a stage I need to reach — letting go of Michelle — and remaining angry at her is holding me back from getting there. This means I'm stuck, at least for now. I'm working on it.

I believe people seek an antidote, a sort of counterbalance to whatever's been causing them pain or unhappiness. If someone's had to endure a high maintenance partner, someone stuck on expensive brands and status symbols, I'd expect them to gravitate next toward some casual, laid-back person. From one extreme to the other.

As for pathologically uptight and rigidly controlling Michelle, what would be her opposite? Someone wild, a free spirit, tending toward earthy, natural and intuitive. That's how I see it.

What about Karl? Even though he's not rebounding from an actual person but from unrestrained bachelorhood, the woman he ends up with will probably be more buttoned-down, organized and conventional in her approach to life. My imagination produces a picture of what Sadie might be like. Maybe a librarian, a schoolteacher or accountant. Someone mature and restrained will be good for Karl.

Yet I can't reconcile this image with the screaming I heard the other night. This disconnect frustrates me.

Every night lately, Karl's gone. It's sad and pathetic, thinking this has anything to do with me. It's Sadie. Of course she's his focus. If I had a woman like her, like I imagine her to be, I'd be doing the same.

This is how my mind goes. Without sleep, thoughts become untethered. Perspective fractures.

I keep trying on Karl's suggestions, but none seem to fit. Maybe I'm resisting. On some level we're opposites, not just different from one another, but incompatible in temperament. I'm trying to shift my priorities and assumptions to conform to those of another man. I'm not sure it's going to work. Maybe instead of being more Karl, I should be more myself. Think of all the ways I've changed since college, since Michelle. Go back to focusing on my own comfort and pleasure, strengthen my own nature rather than weaken it.

It's not some wild party girl I need. That's fine for Karl. Not someone like me.

What kind of woman would I choose, if I could imagine one best suited to me? Someone without my frailty. Strong and defiant, not compromised. A woman who would never waste days in an office surrounded by people who don't respect her. Someone who follows her own desires, rather than lying around worrying, am I appreciated, or will I ever be understood?

I waste too much fucking time worrying about the approval of thoughtless people.

Daylight is coming. Still no sleep. Not even rest.

I want to live on an "idea" level, not a physical level. Art, poetry, philosophy. I used to think Michelle was that way. She possesses a mind, but no heart. She makes calculations about music and poetry, without feeling. I have to create my own design for the life I want to build. Dream whatever I want to be.

But how am I supposed to dream if I can't sleep?

Every part of me is failing. I'm constantly distracted, obsessed with abstractly sexual thoughts. What was I just thinking about testosterone? Michelle stunted me for sure. Twenty-one years married, and I'm almost half a century old, yet I remain a boy. Constantly fearful, half-sexed, semi-masculine. I'm sick of being Michelle's idea of a man. No more.

The sun's coming up. I could call in sick. What did Constant say, back in April? No more sick days. But I don't think he meant not ever again. Wasn't it for ninety days? Better not risk it. Even if Constant needs me, he doesn't realize it, has zero idea what it is I do. Probably thinks anybody out in the yard could do the CAD work and 3D modeling.

No calling in sick, not today. Out of bed. I'm up.

It isn't even 5:30 yet. I stagger into the shower, clean myself up, get dressed. I stare into the mirror. Can't recognize him. Me. It's not the mirror's fault. Those broken eyes. Dying face. Angles out of alignment.

I drive in so early nothing's happening. The graveyard shift is leaving, grease-smeared shipwrights and soot-black welders. They never know what to make of me. I hope at least Constant will get in soon enough to credit me for arriving early.

Nodding at my desk. Can't let myself sleep.

"That's better, Guy," Constant shouts. "Six-fifteen. I like it."

Shit, he's here. Straighten up, turn on my computer. Open some CAD files, zoom the display so the lines on the monitor become abstract. Impossible to tell walking by that these parts fit a fishing trawler we rebuilt nine months ago, and already billed out. Just intersecting lines, inscrutable curves like the diagram of some Da Vinci invention massively expanded.

By nine Constant shuts his office door, leaves for the day. The open plan office is divided into quadrants, with one quarter each for a reception area, then Bookkeeping, Payroll and me. Constant refers to us as the "office girls," which of course gives all the hardhat guys permission to jeeringly repeat this phrase.

Constant has a posh office, windows overlooking the Columbia, three Richard Petty lookalike stock cars, and a couple million in the bank, but he still remains one of the guys. Wears his hardhat when he goes out to the yard, knows how to handle the tools. Even gets his hands dirty every day, though he doesn't need to anymore.

I go to the reception window, check the parking lot for Karl's Firebird. Not there. Karl's one of "the guys" too, chief among them in a sense, though Karl at least has stopped referring to me as one of the "office girls." Out in the yard, without supervision from Karl or Constant himself, twenty-nine guys waste time, shouting and grabassing. Plasma cutters should be sizzling, TIG welders snapping and burning, but no metal's getting cut or fabbed around here. Nothing's getting built.

I stand up. "Going home sick."

Jeannine in Payroll perks up. "You got no sick pay left." She's seventy-seven, with a 1950s platinum bouffant. Jeannine wears pink eye shadow and pink baby doll dresses every day.

"But I'm off ninety-day probation, right?"

"Yeah." Jeannine pops her pink bubble gum. "So you'll take a half-day unpaid then."

"My stomach's really bad." I make a face. "I'll find something for it at the market, then get some sleep."

"When my Benjy gets a bad tummy, I give him Spaghetti-os and ginger ale," Jeannine says. "Not mixed together, I mean. One to eat, one to drink." Benjy is Jeannine's demented husband. He's ninety years old, and thinks Jeannine's a teenage girl. They baby-talk on the phone dozens of times every day.

Before I head out, I email Karl, tell him I'm cutting out, just in case he's planning to show up later.

Jeannine's prescription for Benjy gives me an idea. It's not comfort food I need, or medicine, but something else. I need to feed myself new experiences, new places. Maybe my mind will start to change.

I get home, find Karl's still not around. I change clothes, grab the fishing gear he told me I could keep. This plan feels like withholding something, or keeping a secret. Karl's been nothing but a friend to me. I'm not sure why I feel like I'm being sneaky or deceptive.

I cross the Interstate Bridge into Washington. A half hour later, when the locked gate at the edge of River Road comes into view, I finally admit to myself where I've been going all along.

# Chapter 7

## Alone to the Kalama

The first time Karl brought me here, I arrived with an open mind and no expectations. Now my hands tremble. What is it, anticipation, or a sense of something important looming? Of all the things Karl and I experienced that day, what sticks in my mind most vividly is that last place, the deep, clear pools in the center of that canyon. Fish holding steady, seeming to levitate, hidden from the sun.

On my way up the driveway, carrying my gear, I keep an eye open for signs of anyone else. Though Karl said this man Cayson rarely stayed in the house, still I feel self-conscious, showing up unescorted. At least Karl knows the man, probably well enough to explain his presence if confronted. I wonder how Cayson would take it, if I explained my intrusion by saying I'm the roommate of the son of a dead man who once helped him with a property deal in the Pearl?

I almost expect every detail to have changed from my recollection, but just like before, the house comes into view, imposing and almost certainly vacant. Nothing to worry about, nobody home. At that point in the driveway, the dirt trail cuts away toward the river. Deeper into the trees I feel concealed, safe, invisible. I'm still not exactly sure what I'm seeking, what memory I would revisit, if I could choose. Catching the fish, or enjoying the scenery, the smells, the sounds of birds, or just the hypnotic pleasure derived from the repetitive act of fishing itself. If some aspect of Karl's simple, masculine, unworried nature can be found out here, that's what I might hope to find. I'm actually not even sure I'll be able to manage the tackle without Karl's help. Tie fly to lead, lead to line. I remember Karl repeating this, speaking it like a mantra. Then later, cast, watch the drift, reel in. Cast again.

Vaguely I recall fishing as a boy, though never fly fishing. That cheap Zebco pole and reel, black plastic trimmed with fake chrome. Garish silver and neon spinners attached to hooks. Spinning lures, that's what we called them back then. Sometimes hooks with worms. I must have been eight or ten years old, but I remember almost nothing about that kid. I played baseball, rode my bike, traded comic books with other boys. Crashed in the dirt, scabbed up knees and elbows. I didn't worry much then, but somehow, aging weakened me. I used to be so different.

The trees thin near the river. Birds invisible above, their sounds punctuating the water's murmur. A smell of the sun's warmth on riverbank grass, wafting into the trees.

Rather than go down to this faster-moving water where Karl and I began last time, I turn left, follow the upper bank downstream.

I'm curious about Cayson's big unoccupied house. It's got to be at least three thousand square feet, four or five bedrooms. A lot more house than the one I shared with Michelle, and certainly nice enough to live in full-time. It's strange, a man owning a place like this, and leaving it unoccupied.

Instead of continuing on the trail parallel to the river as planned, I veer back into the trees, toward the house. I want to get a closer look. As the gray painted wood in the distance comes visible through the trees, I slow. No cars outside. No lights. No sign of current presence or recent activity. Once I'm sure I'm alone, I feel a kind of thrill. Like a kid exploring the unknown, venturing into forbidden rooms.

This time I'm not following Karl, going where he says we should go. Now it feels like an adventure.

I creep toward the lower deck, trying to remain quiet, even though I'm convinced I'm the only person for miles. The first window looks into a kitchen, an empty stainless sink, stone countertops. It's a nice enough place, but not so distinct from many of the houses in my old neighborhood. I decide to get down to the river as originally planned.

From the house, the path takes a different cut through the trees, more directly toward the canyon where I landed and released my first steelhead. The landscape here feels wilder, trees older and more substantial than the scattered newer-growth evergreens buffering the house from River Road. Though a trail exists in the direction I intend to go, it's less clearly defined, more grown over with vines and ferns. Moss spreads in thick green cushions up and down tree trunks, and streams loose, hanging from low branches, beginning to dry and fade in summer. The air feels closed off, like the protected, almost subterranean atmosphere in the canyon where I'm headed.

As I walk, I keep an eye on the ground, making sure I don't trip. After a while, the house lost from view behind me, I sense movement to my left. I catch a glimpse of what appears to be a slight figure slipping behind a stout white oak, which stands out among so many evergreens. I stop, unsure of what I saw. The lack of movement or sound make me wonder. It looked like a woman, with long dark hair flowing behind as she ran on tiptoes.

I step nearer the tree, stop and listen again. Stand perfectly still. No movement, just subtle wind, and a light shower of pine needles falling from high overhead. I move to the oak, reach out, place my hand flat on the broad trunk as if to test its solidity. Convinced there's nothing here, I make a circuit, return to where I began. Then I notice what else is different about this tree. Unlike the rest, this trunk isn't thick with moss. Also, shapes and lines are cut into the bark. Thin slashes, like razor cuts in flesh, so subtle I only notice them now that I'm close. The cuts are seeping, more red than amber. This makes the lines resemble bleeding wounds, and I touch one of them, a shape like a rune or ward from old magic. I expect my fingers to come away wet or sticky, but the lines are dry and hard. Looking closer, I see more of these outlines all over the tree, varied sizes and configurations, some ornamented with tiny white seeds or spores stuck in the blood-red sap.

I feel slightly afraid, like I've stumbled upon someone's secret. More than that, my heart pounds with wonder at the beautiful, confusing mystery of this tree. It's something I never would have noticed if I hadn't approached so near.

"Hello?" I call, not expecting any answer. There must not be anyone here. I just circled the tree, found nothing.

A sound, then. Rustling from the opposite side of the trunk.

I hurry around, thinking I'll catch someone scrambling, trying to hide, but there's nobody. Then I notice an opening in the trunk I hadn't seen at first. It's a wide split near the ground, large enough to hide inside. If anyone were hiding there, I could see them. It's just a vacant hollow. But then I hear the sound again, this time coming from within. I kneel, stick my head inside, and look up. Something's definitely moving, up in the black hollow. Without thinking, I plunge my hand up, into the dark. My fingers find something wet and cold. I gag at the smell of rot, like a decomposing animal.

I pull my hand back. Whatever I might have heard, there's nothing here. Nobody. I'm alone.

A chill of fear overtakes me, revulsion at the dark, foul smear covering my hand to the wrist. I stand, back away from the tree, holding my hand behind me so I don't have to smell the organic rot.

Carrying my gear left-handed, I hurry directly toward the water, more interested in washing my hand than anything. The section of river I find in my urgency is neither the rougher upriver stretch where I began, nor the placid downriver canyon pool. Here the water moves not in discrete whirls, eddies and chutes, but as a uniform mass, unhurried but insistent, conveying downstream untold billions of gallons, thousands or perhaps millions of steelhead, along with all other manner of life. Washing my hands, I decide I'll fish here, try this unfamiliar stretch of river between the faster and slower extremes.

When I turn to the shore, open my bag and with dripping hands start to assemble my gear, something on a rock face up the bank stops me. On a smooth, almost perfectly flat stone, like a gray chalkboard angled up to face the sun, someone has scrawled letters and shapes in what must be blood. At first I want to believe this is actually the same reddish sap I just found seeping from the oak, but this is different. The forms are rougher and more primal, not rendered with a careful blade but smeared with hands, like the finger-painting of a reckless child. I can't make sense of the words, maybe Nordic runes or Cyrillic letters, or neither. Although I can't understand, or even articulate the nature of feeling this inspires, the designs are so unpleasant to look at, I change my mind about remaining here to fish. I pick up my gear and resolve to continue downriver toward my original destination, the still pool. As I prepare go, I force myself to take one final look at the awful smeared shapes. They appear to be comprised not only of blood, but fragments of shattered bone and meatier solid matter like the guts of animals or fish.

I hurry up the bank and feel relief, back on the upper trail I recognize. I continue down toward the canyon.

Already I've seen so much of interest, I can't keep it all straight. The empty house. The hollow, decorated tree. Evergreens hung with ancient moss. The stone smeared with symbols. Too much to remember, though I know these details will spin through my mind until I understand them.

In the place where Karl stopped before, I find the gap, push through, and descend into the canyon. Here are my footprints and Karl's, undisturbed since our visit. Exactly as I expect, a cluster of steelhead hover in water so clear it seems invisible. Each casts a shadow on the floor of the pool. I have the same uncanny sense of witnessing levitation in air. This place feels wild, timeless, almost primal. Protected down in this valley below the rest of the world, it seems to be hidden from the sun, and from all eyes above.

Without my conscious awareness of what I'm doing, my hands have assembled the components of my fishing gear. Fly to lead to line, easy and nimble, as if I've done this a thousand times. Though in reality I've only fished the once with Karl, in my mind I've done this many times, a sort of practice in imagination.

I face the water and cast, witness the line's slow drift, and finally reel in. This repeats several times, a rhythmic extension of my reach far beyond the grasp of arms and hands, until I release the line with a flick and it carries to the point my eyes have chosen. The end of the process leads back to the beginning, and goes on forever. I remember everything Karl said, without realizing it's something I ever learned. So meditative, peaceful. Not sure that's how Karl experiences it, but that's how it feels to me, especially now that I'm alone. My mind clears, motionless and transparent as the water.

My reverie breaks at a wild splash. First I think someone's dived into the pool from above, scattered the fish, then I become mindful of tension on my line. A living thing flutters, pulling sideways beneath the water. I draw back, try to set the hook, then modulate the pressure against the fish to prevent it throwing the hook. Pull, reel a few times, then pull some more. Don't hurry, but don't let up. My heart thumps wildly, all primal fear and excitement, so much more visceral than when Karl was here. I'm not sure why I should be afraid, but the idea of losing the fish, of failing to bring it in, alarms me more than any other possible failure I might imagine.

Sweat drips down my face, my neck and back. Coming in closer, the steelhead continues its swerving, left to right, downstream and back up. I bring it nearer. When it's almost to the bank, I remember Karl swooping in with his net, but I don't think I have one. I keep tension, sidestep nearer my bag, and shoot a glance to make sure.

The gear Karl gave me definitely doesn't include a net. What would Karl do?

I can let it go, or keep what I've caught. I can take it home. What feels right to me, natural? I don't want to repeat what happened before.

Determined not to freeze up, to let the chance slip, I reach for the little weighted bat. Reel in and lift, work the exhausted fish until it's right in front of me. My left hand grasps the steelhead by the tail, holds it steady. Right hand grasps the bat handle and swings.

I strike the fish on the side of the head. Blood sprays, the body stiffens, then relaxes straight. At this outcome, I become aware of possibilities within me, previously submerged potential. When I think of before, my too-cautious handling of the earlier fish, I feel angry.

I rest the fish on the gravel at the water's edge, and go back for another look in the gear bag. What else is there? A folding knife, gray metal, like a weapon for killing. I unfold the blade and slit the steelhead lengthwise, down the belly. I remember seeing this before, maybe in a movie. Pull out loose innards, blood spilling over my hands, clutching the remains of this thing which lived only a minute ago. Pride, revulsion, both at once. I fling the guts out into the water. Some of the mess flies wildly from my hand and lands on the rocks of the bank. The resulting pattern of this accidental mess resembles what I left behind not long ago, up river. What have I made? A question mark in entrails? An exclamation point? Blood all over my hands, I feel a bit deranged, theatrical and wild-eyed after the killing and gutting. I'm breathing heavily, invigorated. It feels good, I think.

This is a ceremony, a summoning. What else do I want? What could I wish for?

I consider walking back to the car just like this. There's something weirdly satisfying about the blood and the smell I now carry, but I decide I'd better wash my hands. What might work here in this primeval canyon wouldn't look right, driving my car back to the city. I swirl hands in the water, rub one against the other. The blood disperses, strangely milky in the water. The smell is wild and strange, not merely fish or blood but something more. By the time I rinse the gutted steelhead, the other fish are already beginning to return to the pool. This makes no sense to me, though it does bring to mind what Karl said. Catch one, pull him from the water, and the rest will spook and scatter. But right away they forget how afraid they were. The commotion dies down and they fall right back into their holding pattern. Karl said sometimes he might catch the same fish again and again, pull out the hook and see another hole in its mouth where an hour before, he hooked and released the same fish.

One minute it's the end of the world, the next it's like nothing ever happened.

Maybe I'm like that. I forget trouble sooner than I should, put myself back in harm's way. I should finally learn and stop coming back.

I wrap the cleaned fish in a ratty paper sack from the bottom of my gear bag. The watery smell of fish soaks through the paper. I stow my gear, wash my hands one last time. I can still smell everything that happened, still feel my heart crashing inside of my chest.

I stand on the bank a while, trying to calm myself. This smooth surface, I could watch forever.

Eventually I pick up my gear and scramble back up the bank. Have to go back to the world.

When I reach the top and emerge through the brush, the sky has turned from blue to steel gray. It's like emerging into a world I thought I might never see again. I walk that edge, teetering between forest and river, until I reach a tangle of spiny blackberry canes taller than myself.

Beyond this barrier is a clearing in the trees, the grass field with an A-frame house in the center. It's the one I saw before, but more rustic than I remember. In fact, many details seem different from my recollection. The timbers are raw and unfinished, angles slightly off, as opposed to my memory of a place more modern and refined.

Last time, I saw a woman there, outside the house. What if she's here again? There's nothing wrong with admitting to myself that I've been imagining her, trying to recreate a mental picture of how she appeared as I walked by. I'm fighting against the idea I should force myself to behave in some way different from my true nature, or that I should want anything other than what I want. My impulses are worth something. This heaviness that's been burdening me everywhere I go, an ennui, it's no longer just sadness over losing

Michelle. That transient loss has evolved into a sense of permanent futility, one it's up to me to break.

Don't fret so much over whether or not that woman is here, or worry in advance about what I might say. That will ruin it. If my focus becomes too intense, or preconceptions too specific, nothing will ever come to pass. If it doesn't happen, I'll just have to go home, clean myself up, and get some sleep. Start on a better tomorrow.

Still I feel tension around my eyes, in my forehead. My jaw clenches. What the hell's wrong with me? Try to relax. I shake my head, hoping to loosen my neck. I crouch behind the blackberry canes, squeezing my eyes shut, trying to clear my mind.

A door creaks open.

I straighten and look.

The woman stands motionless outside the door. I can't tell if she sees me, hiding at the edge of her field. Something in the shape of her, the length of her neck and angle of her jawline, reminds me of Michelle. I'm not sure what she's wearing, some kind of cloth wrap, an unusual kind of dress. Her hair is casual, almost messy, but appealing. She seems out of place in these wild surroundings, as if she arrived moments before from some downtown restaurant or art gallery and hasn't yet realized her surroundings have changed. That incongruity should bother me, would normally frustrate my desire to categorize, but at this moment I'm intrigued.

I start walking up the trail through the field, as if I have nothing in mind but to walk back to my car. The tension in my hunched shoulders is too great, and I have to stop. I make an effort to lower the tackle and pole I'm carrying, to relax. Just start again. Walk naturally.

She's not watching me. Not even looking at me.

The woman seems younger than me, but not too young. It's hard to tell. Her hair is almost black, that much is clear. At first I think she's hanging laundry on a line tied between the house and a pole, but I look closer and see there's no laundry, and no pole. She's doing something with rope up against the side of the house, looping and tying. She reaches, stands on tiptoe, lifts one bare foot, sole green from the grass. I wonder, does this place have running water, or is it just for camping? How does she wash clothes, or bathe?

She wipes her forehead, pushes strands of dark hair back from her eyes. Then she turns, catches me watching her, and sets down what she's working on. Her face lightens, almost a smile. "Any luck?"

It seems like no time at all has passed since I first walked by and saw her here, but of course this isn't true. It's just that I haven't stopped thinking about her since then, without really admitting it to myself until now. She's been on my mind the whole time I fished, so in a sense, we've been having a conversation all along. Caught up in these thoughts, I hesitate several seconds before I register what she's said.

I raise the gear slightly. "Fishing you mean? I'm just learning." I've veered slightly off the trail, toward her. Nearer.

She takes a few steps nearer me as well, until we're less than twenty feet apart. She raises arms to her sides, stretching. "So you didn't catch anything?"

"I did."

She looks neither approving nor disapproving.

"You live out here?" I ask. "Or are you camping?"

She lowers her arms, wraps them around herself. "I come to work."

Slowly I take two steps closer, stop again. "Then maybe I'll see you next time."

"Be careful there." She gestures toward the trees, into which the trail vanishes. "It's getting dark."

This suggestion surprises me, until I look up to the sky. She's right. The sun is hidden below the horizon, and dark gray clouds have come in. What time is it?

I have to go. We nod and wave, and I start walking again.

The last mile blurs.

Who am I, out here pretending to fish, walking through another man's forest?

Who is this woman, living like this, alone in a field?

I'm alone now, but feel like I've just spent a rewarding day with someone newly important to me. Part of this must be the afterglow of my time out on the river, and landing my own fish. This invigorating sense of grasping hold of new possibilities. It's also more than that. I feel a sense of belonging, almost of partnership, like when I was married. This makes no sense, I realize. It can't possibly have anything to do with this woman. We barely spoke. But it feels compelling, too urgent and real to dismiss completely.

When I reach my car, I realize I don't remember most of the walk. I've been distracted. Compared to all the details I noticed on my way in, nothing registered on my return trip. The diagonal trail past the vacant house. The last half of the gravel drive. Looming evergreens swaying. I imagine these things as I saw them before, can populate a believable vision out of memory, full of the smells of river and sounds of birds. But these details are from before, not now.

"I'm actually here," I whisper, climbing through the barrier gate. "Remember this."

I unlock my car. The interior lights up, I stow my gear in back and climb in behind the wheel. The dashboard clock says nine-thirty. Everything around me is black, the sky, the forest. Allowing for a thirty minute walk each way, that means I fished more than ten hours. That's impossible. It seemed less than two, even counting the digression toward the house, the strange oak, and the stretch of the river where I didn't stay long. When I was done fishing and left the canyon, the sun was still high. Then I saw the woman, and I'm sure she cast a shadow against the front of her house. I only lingered a minute.

But when she warned me it was getting dark, it seemed perfectly right, a logical observation following on from whatever we were discussing. I didn't question her, at first.

Though the hours don't add up, I feel tired enough for nine-thirty. I'm hesitant to turn the key, afraid the car won't start, that I've emerged into some imposter world, everything replaced. Michelle is gone, my job doesn't exist, there is no houseboat with Karl. All around me feels strange, disaster imminent.

My key turns, the ignition fires. The engine revs exactly like usual. Nothing's wrong.

# PART 2

# A

# TRANSFORMATION

# Chapter 8

## Sleep evades what never rests

After so many broken nights, I fear sleep is a habit lost forever. The worst thing, the most torturous mockery of my cumulative fatigue, is after I've endured a work day barely functional, focused on nothing but my desire to stagger home and finally rest, then five o'clock finally comes. I make it home, draw curtains and climb straight into bed, burying myself beneath mounds of bedding to protect my eyes against invasive light. I only want to collapse. Such a relief to relax, to give in.

Then nothing comes.

I struggle to remain still, eyelids pressed shut, ignore the sound of the river flowing, deny thoughts of what must be happening out in the still day-lit world. Don't worry about my job, avoid comparing it to occupations of college friends and other people Michelle and I used to know. Try not to consider the notion that some brighter profession, or more money, might have helped sustain Michelle's interest. Instead lie frozen in this void, stuck between my obsolete past and some future I can't yet identify. Neither fully awake nor dreaming. What is this state of mind? Not reverie. Nothing so pleasant as daydream.

I've fallen into the habit of blaming Michelle for inflicting all my damage, but lying here, anxious heart pounding, I can't deny that my weaknesses must predate her. I can't remember where or when things started to break. Too long ago.

No emotions any more. Just obsessions, mental loops and meanderings.

Water is constantly flowing, whether or not I remain mindful. Not only the Columbia below me, stretching beyond my window. Also a narrower stream in another place, a channel beneath soil, hidden from prying eyes. What cleared this one spot amid miles of forest? Imagine hundreds of years ago, maybe thousands, settlers or natives cutting trees, clearing space for a sort of village. Room to graze animals, plant vegetables. Nearby, a river thick with coho and Chinook salmon and steelhead. Fresh, clean water without end. That's how it was, how it must have been.

A great forest cut by a single river. Ancient trees shield all but the circle. Even Cayson's home remains hidden.

Under that sky I might recline, see stars blinking against light of lost eons.

Blood. Whose blood on my hands? Not my own. My blood is stuck inside veins. It wants out. It churns, makes noise the way a river flows. Maybe that's the roaring in my ears.

My life is a tumble of wrecked metal. I used to be smarter, could decide which path deserved following. If anything bad came along, I'd cut it loose. What do I have left that's any good? A single shelf of books; seventeen, a prime number. I don't want to purchase the same books again, duplicate my old collection. What if I moved on, re-purchased everything I used to own, then Michelle admitted she was wrong? I'd move back and have two copies of everything. Do I want that future, a double collection to remind me forever that Michelle made me leave, and that I crawled back?

I'll only buy books that are new to me. Someday Michelle will see the things I've discovered. Or else she won't.

I have wishes, but my problem is, none of them are likely to come true.

What do I wish for? No more nights like this. I'm tired of burning with envy for every other person in this world.

# Chapter 9

### Frame without a picture

On my way out the front door to work, feeling dazed from fatigue, I stumble over an envelope held up against the exterior by a leaning cinderblock. I pick it up. A letter from Michelle, apparently hand-delivered. This elicits not hope or excitement, but a feeling of overwhelming exhaustion. Also, slightly delayed, a trace of self-congratulation for not being pleased to hear from her for a change. At least this gives me hope I'm in the process of setting aside my past.

I don't read the letter, don't even open it, but fold the envelope in half and carry it in my pocket. Maybe later.

At work, I'm not surprised to find Karl isn't there again. Lately he's missed quite a few days, in fact hasn't even been home in such a long time, I've lost track. On one hand this seems kind of alarming, but I know I shouldn't worry. He seems focused on his girlfriend. Probably they're at her place every night.

During the lunch break, even though I plan to eat at my desk, I venture into the break room to buy a Cherry Coke. Really I'm curious to see if Constant says anything, so I linger by the corner where he's holding court.

Constant sees me. "Too bad about our boy." His mouth splits into a gap-filled uneven grin. All the hardhats call him "Hollywood," because of this uneven ragged smile, and his clownish red hair which stands out in every direction. I used to think the crazy hair was an affectation, at least an attempt to be funny, then I realized he simply doesn't care. The nasty mouth is strange, though. Constant may come from a working-class background, but he's pretty well off now, and we have good health and dental insurance.

Anyway, Constant thinks they call him Hollywood because of all his expensive cars.

"Karl, you mean?" I act surprised.

"You seen him this morning?" he asks. "Ain't he at home?"

I have to guess how to play this. "He said he felt lousy and might have to call in."

Constant looks suspicious. "Brown bottle flu, maybe, Monday after all those weekend plans?"

I want to ask what he knows of Karl's weekend, but can't reveal that I have no idea myself. Instead I do what Karl would. I shrug. Constant loses interest, so I leave the break room and return to my desk.

Quickly I compose an email to Karl's personal account, in case Constant has someone checking Karl's work inbox.

*Subject: Are you okay?*

*Message: Constant's not happy. Get back in here if you can.*

I'm about to click send.

"What the fuck's this shit?" Constant squawks behind me.

I spin, resisting the urge to cover my screen.

He's not looking at my computer display, but a pair of photos on my cubicle wall. I'd forgotten them, framed photographic prints of abstract water textures, hung at least five years ago. He pokes one with a greasy fingertip, and I'm glad they're under glass. Constant's hands always stink like transmission fluid. I think he likes the smell, applies it like cologne.

"Water photographs," I say. "They're textural."

"God fucking damn, Guy, you want to see water, we'll get you a job outside, there." He points toward his office or more likely the boat yard beyond it. "Don't you already got enough fucking river, boy?"

Constant has always been kind of a bully. He enjoys selecting people to give a hard time who can't talk back. Today, at least, I figured he might leave me alone, since Karl must be on his list with so many recent absences. I should know better. Now that I live with Karl, his attendance problems reflect on me, too.

Even after Constant returns to his office, irritation remains. I feel like an outcast here, worse than ever since Karl's gone. Just one of the office girls. Of course I'm feeling sorry for myself, but not a lot is going right for me at the moment. I used to have a wife who seemed to get me, though obviously she didn't. I have a roommate who's almost a friend, but he's gone too. Otherwise I'm surrounded by men slick with grease and stinking of chemicals, so rough they make Karl seem like an English butler. They shout what they mean, snatch what they want, and if sometimes their hand gets slapped away, they only laugh.

I need to clear my head, get focused. There's more than enough work to keep me busy, at least for a while. I won't wonder about Karl, or imagine seeing his girlfriend in the dark, or picture the strange woman in the field. Just to make sure I avoid distractions, I shut down email, turn my back on my main computer, and instead focus on the dedicated CAD workstation on my side desk. The work I do at Constant Marine isn't something just anyone could manage, but the truth is, since I've become familiar with the AutoCAD program tools and shortcuts, and understood the basic concepts, it doesn't exactly require all my mental focus. Actually, I wish it demanded more. The days would go by faster.

In no time, the first design is done. I consider starting work on the next, but decide I need a break.

Outside, the welders sizzle and pop. Usually when Karl's gone, nothing happens. Constant must have gone out and raised hell, gotten them started putting something together. I scroll up the production schedule, try to guess what they're building.

Sometimes I hate this cubicle. Gray fabric walls, a soft prison. A padded cell.

Still no word from Karl. It's stupid of me, worrying like this. I wasn't going to think about him.

I need to change things up, start some new routine, shift my sense of self. I feel a little stronger, more self-assured. How can I really cement this new beginning? Maybe change the way I dress at work, or how my desk is decorated. These things may seem superficial, but they're the frame that surrounds much of my daily life. I still have photos of Michelle on my desk. That's fucking depressing. I sit here pretending I don't look at those pictures five hundred times a day. My ex-wife, still front and center.

Time for something new.

I turn one of the frames face-down on the desk, slide out the back and remove the photo. I don't have any new pictures I want to put inside, that's the problem. All these frames, Michelle on all sides, and I've got nothing new worth replacing them. I slide the empty frame back together, stand it up in the same spot. It's ugly, looks cheap, but at least this way I know I'll remember to find something new to replace it. I repeat the process with the other Michelle photos, replace empty frames, throw prints in the trash. Then I place a blank sheet from a legal pad on top of the photos so I don't have to see her looking up at me.

A few minutes later I take the pictures back out of the trash and put them inside my drawer, face down. By three o'clock, all I've accomplished, other than an hour of CAD work on fixtures and joints for that 5086 H321 aluminum project, is moving around photos of my ex-wife. Now the only thing in my trash is that single plain sheet of paper I used to cover the photos.

Never mind. I'll give some more thought to redecorating my cubicle, and consider another idea. Maybe start eating different lunches. No. I'm thinking too small.

That blank paper in the trash keeps bugging me. I roll my chair over, lean in, grab it.

My cell phone rings. It's Karl. I answer without speaking his name.

"What's the problem?" he asks. "That loony email you sent."

"Just letting you know what's up." I let the yellow sheet flutter back into the trash. "You've been gone a lot."

"Yeah. And I won't be home for a bit."

"Must be nice." I spin into jealousy. It's stupid, but I can't help it. Just imagining what it must be like, avoiding work, and getting to know someone new.

"Something wrong, Tiger?"

"What? Why?"

"You sound pissed, is all."

"Ah... Just Constant, giving me trouble again." Though the boss hasn't said anything today to upset me, I dredge up something from a few days ago, because I don't want Karl knowing he's the one who's actually got me irritated. I keep my raspy imitation of Constant down to a whisper. *"Ever since Michelle kicked your ass out, your attitude's for shit. Always coming in bug-eyed hung-over, and smart-assing me."*

"He's right about the bug-eyed part."

"Fuck off, Karl. At least I'm here."

"Just trying to help a fella, Tiger. You need to get laid, relax, and get some sleep. Total reboot."

It pisses me off, hearing nothing from Karl for days, then he immediately starts in with telling me how I need to be more like him. "Fuck off with your stupid advice."

"Anyway, you got the place to yourself. Jack off in the living room if you want. Actually, never mind, don't get on my sofa with that shit."

I want to ask where he's been, and about the girlfriend. I consider telling Karl what I saw that night, the dark, his door left open. I remember, even if he doesn't. While I debate whether I should, Karl signs off, hangs up.

Back to my PC. the production list. I don't feel like drawing fixtures any more. I get up and walk outside, down the edge of the parking lot and around behind Constant's office. I find the corner of the yard with the best view of the river, away from solvent fumes and smoke from welding and plasma cutting. Also, the lowest likelihood of grit-caked meatheads bothering me.

I take out Michelle's letter.

It's shorter than I expect, just a single page, one-sided. Expensive textured cotton stationery. The ridiculous thing is, despite everything that's happened, the sight of her handwriting makes me think I might actually start to cry. I put the letter back in my pocket until this idea passes. Anger helps. Fucking engaged, so stupid. I breathe slow and deep, looking out across the water.

I pull out the letter again. This time I'll get through it, no problem.

The note is a sort of catalog, a series of points justifying Michelle's point of view, rationalizing a string of disparate acts as if they're somehow connected. Root causes of her withholding of intimacy. Why I had to leave the house. The reason divorce was the only answer. Her suggestion I keep paying the mortgage. The logic by which my books and CDs became hers. There's nothing in the letter about her recent engagement. Maybe she recognizes it for the doomed, irrational gesture it clearly is.

Michelle hopes I grasp her hopes, her intentions. I used to believe I did. Now, having read this note, I wonder.

One sentence sticks. "I will always love you, but can never say those words face-to-face or even on the phone, because I know you would misunderstand them as a kindness."

After, I'm able to see my ex-wife from a new, completely unfamiliar vantage point. This involves a bizarre sense of disorientation, following so many conversations, so much living, almost a quarter century of relationship and intimacy, and even these recent months of abjection, to become abruptly aware how delicate it all is, and must always have been. Maybe all I've ever needed to grant me this perspective was to read a letter like this one.

Yes, she's struggling to understand herself, to act her way toward life's next chapter. Wonderful. In that sense, we're the same. So why does this letter infuriate me? Why this uprising of anger toward myself, rather than her? Though I understand some of what she's trying to convey, it doesn't matter. She waited to share these secrets until they were no longer any use to me.

I stand at the corner of this rectangle of land studded with cranes and man-lifts, stacks of rusting steel plate and heavy chain, ranks of gear for welding, cutting, grinding. Beyond this, the wide river moves. I dare myself to cry, sincerely wish it to happen. I want this out of me, want to heave it up and feel cleansed. But no tears will come.

# Chapter 10

### A flow that never ends

When I return to the office, I feel changed. Cubicle walls can't touch me. I wonder if it shows, this transformation of mine.

Day shift hardhats stream into the office, punch out and leave for home. Payroll and HR follow. I'm anxious to get away too, but I'm waiting until Constant leaves, just because I'm trying to support the impression that I'm always reliably at my desk. Then I realize he must've already gone while I was outside, and just left his office light on. I switch it off, shut his door. I'm alone here.

On my way out it occurs to me that while I'm ready to leave, I don't actually want to go home. What else is there? As I near a front window made reflective by security spotlights, I approach someone who resembles me, but his eyes are dark, and a smear of blood obscures his mouth.

"Who the fuck?" I gasp, startled, and reflexively reach for my lips.

The reflection does the same. It's me. Fingers come away clean.

Out in my car, I lock myself in and angle the rear-view mirror to check my face. My skin is pale, almost transparent. Black circles under my eyes. I look sick, but there's no visible blood.

I need to change how I sustain myself. Not just food and sleep, but other ways. Unfamiliar pleasures, smells. New music and books. I'm not Karl. Instead of trying to be less myself, I should be more.

On Marine Drive, instead of turning left toward home, turn right toward I-5, then south into the city. I park off Burnside on NW 22nd, in the shadow of the first apartment building Michelle and I lived in when we returned to Portland after college. I explore 23rd as far as north as Lovejoy, come back on 21st, then head down Glisan toward the Pearl. Our old neighborhood is changed, though I've visited here lately enough it's not a complete surprise. I wander past restaurants, boutiques and coffee shops, letting ideas settle.

Drawn by smells into a new shop, *Parfum de Nuit,* I pick up candles scented with cardamom and bitter mandarin, cactus and vetiver, or clove and amber, colored orange, umber, green and gold. Next, incenses named "Fire Soil" and "Mystery of Night Skin." The woman behind the counter suggests a pale green cologne that smells of neroli, tart lime and white pepper. I can't read the bottle, but the scent makes me feel awake and excited. The proprietor says it's perfect for me. She pronounces the name, which I fail to catch, but I don't want to tell her I didn't understand.

Down to the tea vendor, where I find a gold cast iron Japanese tea pot covered with symbols, tins of *pu erh* and matcha teas, a local unsweet chai blend, and a hard-packed brick comprised of sticky clove, nettle and raspberry leaf.

Most of the music stores I used to visit are gone, but Everyday Music survives on Burnside and 14th, up the street from Powell's Books where I plan to stop last. It's hard to find music that means anything to me without being reminded of Michelle. That's my fault, that excess of interconnection. I settle on Michael Nyman's soundtracks for *The Cook, The Thief, His Wife and Her Lover,* and *The Draughtsman's Contract.* I'm on my way to the register, but go back for Steve Reich's *Music for Eighteen Musicians* and LaMonte Young's *Music On a Long Thin Wire.* Each step in my process of selection feels like a deliberate act of tiptoeing through the milestones of Michelle's opinions, moving past them.

In line to pay, I murmur aloud, "I want my own."

In Powell's I find a tattered paperback of Russell Edson's surrealist prose poems, an affordable full-color Taschen edition of Joan Miró art reproductions and history, an ancient hardcover

English translation of *Icelandic Sagas*, and a real treasure, Karl Jung's *Mysterium Coniunctionis*, which blends the subjects of alchemy and psychology. I'm ready to begin anew, with these items forming the blocks of my foundation. Michelle wouldn't buy any of these things, nor would Karl.

On my way out of Powell's, my mind drifts to the woman I saw by the river. I've been thinking of her a lot in a directionless, nonspecific way. I guess I imagine her a sort of counterbalance to Michelle, an unencumbered and mysterious antidote to all my wife's unnecessary complications and self-contradictions. As I push through swinging doors out to the sidewalk, I see her standing there. This can't be her, but it is. I recognize everything, and she seems to recognize me. I want to address her, but don't know her name. I'm about to try to justify myself, to grasp at her before she turns away, explain that we've seen each other before. We've spoken. Don't you remember, I'm about to ask. In that field among the trees, between the Kalama River and Colson's place?

Someone else pushes out of the door behind me, a freckled mother dragging twin children past me by the hands. They pass between us. I still haven't spoken and I'm thinking there's still time, she's here, we're both here, but the intrusion breaks that initial connection.

Once the freckled mother and children are past, the dark haired woman looks at me again, and the friendly recognition I imagined I saw is entirely absent. Her face is different, unfamiliar. Not her. She was never here. This was always someone else.

"Sorry," I murmur, but she's already gone.

I walk away, heading west toward my car. Where else to go? I want to buy more than I can afford, find some new clothes, but my circumstances are limited. Next month I'll return. I have to begin slowly. It's up to me what kind of person I become. Not Michelle. If I just lay around waiting for her to pick me up off the ground, I'm in for a long wait. I have to make an effort. What kind of idiot doesn't at least try to rebuild himself?

I'm surprised how late it is when I get home. I should be hungry, but all I want is to sort through the things I bought.

Candles, tea, music, books. I spread everything out, cover my bed. I want to lie among everything, absorb the smells, but I think I may actually be able to sleep.

I put the new books on the shelf beside the seventeen I managed to rescue from Michelle. Now I have twenty-one. I undress, turn off lights, put on the Reich CD. Everything is dark, not only my room. Only river sounds, until the quiet music begins.

Once I'm in bed, I keep thinking someone's here, like that other night. Karl's gone. She's here. Don't think about it.

I climb out of bed, creep into the hallway, push open Karl's door. This is how it was before. Not trying to intrude, just recreating conditions. Reach into the bathroom, flick on the switch, and watch reflected light spill into the hall.

A woman on the edge of the bed, feet together. She was there before. Not now.

Arrange it all the way it was. Balance light and dark, doors open and closed. I might bring her back, if everything's exactly the same. The sound of screaming. I thought it was pleasure.

I flick off the bathroom light and return to bed. Stop worrying about it. Just need to lie down.

When I was little and couldn't sleep, my mom told me, *Just lie still, rest your eyes.* It's supposed to be better to remain motionless and quiet in the dark. I doubt that's true. Every night I lie here, trying to rest, straining to keep my eyes closed. Then in the morning I feel like exhausted death and have to drag myself to work. Immobility is no help. Parents only say that about resting eyes and keeping quiet so kids will shut up and leave them alone.

I want to tell myself the same. Shut up. Stop crying. Leave me alone.

Nobody's listening.

Sometimes I catch thoughts conforming to strange shapes, blueprints imposed from outside myself. I believe I'm following a clear train of thought, that time is ticking past one second at a time. Then I realize something must've skipped. I've fallen asleep, reawakened. Or maybe everything has jumped far ahead and left me behind. Whatever mechanism keeps track, enforces forward movement, tallies sleeping and wakefulness, mine's somehow broken.

Think about thinking.

Listen to the sound of listening.

Try not to try to sleep.

These processes disconnect and work at cross purposes. Dream of thinking, dream of listening, dream of insomnia. I'm wondering why I can't conjure from imagination the primal sexuality of an unknown woman's cries. I'm not here. I'm somewhere else. That's all fantasy is.

Create a new life. Pour myself into it.

There's a sound from somewhere outside my room. I leap out of bed, go back to the door, look out. Lights are still off. Nobody's moving. Only the river.

I open my eyes and find I'm still in bed. I never got up, only thought I did. This loop is going to kill me.

# Chapter 11

## Faces clearly remembered yet never actually seen

This is actually not a dream. This is my inescapable obsession, a catalog of details from a possible future. If I choose correctly, things can still be set right. I only need to assemble the appropriate objects, component parts of my next self. What alternative do I have? What other end?

All along, I never considered the idea of killing myself. Lately, these merged-together nights, the possibility keeps repeating, an unwanted suggestion offered in a flat, toneless voice. I'm interested in specific details, a visual fantasia like an endless, garish slide show.

I'll use the knife Karl gave me. That grim old utilitarian hunk of steel, fragrant of blood and oil and decades-old rust. Slice open my belly, split myself apart and scoop out my insides. Offer my guts to the river.

What shape will I—

I use the blade without testing it first, find it sharp. I'm willing to cut.

Something dead floats away.

Blood on the ground, taste it in my mouth. Sticky hands, smeared lips. What is the source of this endlessly flowing blood? I hear rushing, a hot current. In the night, women float past, dark faces indistinct. Try to imagine details.

Michelle's long auburn hair tied back straight. Lips pursed around a tart secret.

In her place a taller blond whose face keeps shifting, unresolved. This is the shape from Karl's room, a woman I know because I've imagined her, though we've never met. Her body just an outline, details withheld by darkness. Her face invisible.

She doesn't belong to—

Another, new and different. What form will she take, my own design? She hides among trees, sleeps beside water, waits for me beneath open sky. She asks questions without words. Hair dark, eyes large, skin pale. We chose each other. Been waiting so long, holding on for some impetus outside myself. An offered invitation, or unequivocal arrival onstage.

Yes, I would give my blood.

Say it aloud, say I'll risk for you, I'll offer trade. Possess, devour.

Don't go yet, she says. Not until—

I wake, speaking around her essence, trying to conjure the lost name from a sound. Keep repeating the idea of her, circle around. Declare myself, stand forward. Fear can't resist forever the pull of desire.

The knife is so sharp.

# Chapter 12

### Drawn to the gap between trees

I'm driving before sunrise. No reason justifies such an early start. The cold, brittle morning hints at summer's end. Autumn will clear everything away.

Outside the barrier at the end of Cayson's driveway, birds speak their strange cries, scattering from high atop trees, heaving dense wings into flight. The sky becomes gray as the sun emerges behind an atmosphere heavy with mist. Prior visits, I remember different sounds. Places transform depending on hour or season. Minds change. In various stages of life, we switch between worlds, each as dissimilar from the last as the difference between waking life and dreams.

As I start up the gravel drive that cuts between narrow evergreens, I contemplate my plan for the day. Places I intend to go, events I hope might occur. First, to the river.

Why is it so hard to admit I want to see the woman again? Last time I came here, she was on my mind, but I never let myself admit it. When I finally faced her, only a few words were said. Too soon it was over. There should be no shame in admitting what I'm after. Fear is exhilarating, also empowering. I hope I find her, and if I do, I'll be first to speak. I want to know her name, want to look at her steadily, without flinching. See what she really looks like. It's too early now, but I'll go later, after fishing. That gives me plenty of time to prepare. When the right moment arrives, I'll find her outside. She'll know I'm coming. She'll be waiting.

Where Cayson's house comes into view, I leave the driveway and head toward the more active upper section of river where Karl first took me. I want to avoid the house, vaguely concerned someone might be home, though of course the barrier gate was locked. Whatever it was I saw last time near the house, I don't know how to categorize it. Maybe that's what I'm avoiding, the uncertainty of a figure darting, seeming to hide behind a thick oak. Then my realization the bark was adorned with carved lines. Reaching up into the hollow. Something wet inside. The powerful smell of death.

I realize I'm carrying both sides of a conversation. It seems crazy, worrying so much over a small thing like talking to a woman. How complicated can it be? I know what Karl would say. Just demonstrate my interest, and see what develops.

This is what I'm doing, psyching myself up and at the same time trying to convince myself it's no big deal.

It's only when I see the river I realize I'm not carrying my fishing gear. Must be still in the car. I turn, intending to go back and get it, then doubt stops me. Did I even bring it along? Maybe I left everything at home.

I'm here. I'm not going away. Anyway, I didn't really come to fish. But this changes my plan for the day. At the very least I can locate the field again, get another look at her house, then maybe go down beside the river and think about what to do. I have to be careful she doesn't see me yet, not until I'm ready. I veer downstream toward the canyons, following the river. I don't want to go too far into the trees, or near the house. The trail winds along that strip of thin forest, then sharply curves. I recognize a wild barrier of blackberry canes overtaking a rock mound.

Beyond this is her field.

I pause, have to get control of my thoughts. I'm afraid she might hear what I'm thinking, discern my intentions.

"Don't be crazy," I whisper. My voice cracks.

I'm shivering, my arms prickling with goosebumps. It's barely September. The sun will come later, burn off the clouds. For now, it's freezing.

Right past this verge, I'll just sneak a look, then decide. What's so hard, admitting you want to see someone? Maybe she'll think it's strange that I came here not to fish, but just to see her. No, stop worrying. I have to talk to her. No going back now.

The field appears transformed, so much that I wonder if this is even the right place. The location is correct, relative to the driveway, the house and the river, but the geometry feels less flat and open than what I pictured. I feel a sense of convergence, of being surrounded by walls. It's the heavy, dark ocean of forest behind, focusing all attention toward the center. It's as if this field exerts gravity in all directions, draws everything inward from all sides, even from above. The ground drops away into the middle of the field, almost like a bowl. The roof of the A-frame is lower than the ground on which I'm standing, as if this field is sinking away, possibly trying to conceal itself from those who pass by.

Maybe that's how Karl missed it.

I'm standing on an edge, feeling I might fall in. It's not really a house, more a cabin, smaller, rougher and less finished than the picture I carry in my mind. Halved trees lashed together, all rustic gaps and seams. How does she keep out the rain? It never rains here. Summer never ends.

One moment I'm standing here contemplating the landscape and the house itself, and the next moment, she's outside, looking at me. Her face seems unnaturally white, framed by straight black hair that falls past her shoulders and ends in blunt bangs above arched eyebrows. I've seen her before, yet each element surprises me, as if I don't expect to find her looking quite as she does. Real, not a picture. Out in the middle of nowhere, wearing dark pants and a jacket with a high collar, almost like a uniform.

Only then do I realize I'm standing in plain sight, having stepped too far past the corner barrier to remain hidden. It's that gravity, pulling me in, though I intended to stand back. There's no more time to plan what I might want to say. She sees me. An instant's glance reveals everything, irrevocably. She wants me to approach. I know this as if she's beckoning, but without any movement at all. For an instant I question whether this is right. What I'm seeing doesn't quite compute. She's not surprised to see me, doesn't seem alarmed. She looks like someone getting ready to commute to work.

Before I've consciously made the decision to approach, I find myself already walking. I stop just past the spot where I stopped before. She's standing in exactly the place I expect. It's as if I have a chance to replay our prior meeting.

"You again." Her voice washes over me like relief. No judgment, no surprise at my coming.

I reach for the right words, but nothing comes. I grasp for any observation, a reason to extend the moment. At least learn her name. I think of Karl, feel him watching me, judging yet also encouraging. I have to break through. When I'm fearful, I'm nothing. It cripples me.

The set of her mouth shifts. Her eyes soften. I believe she reads my thoughts, knows my intentions and approves of them, yet recognizes that I'm stuck. She doesn't want anyone timid.

I can get past this. These doubts are my own, self-imposed. I don't want them anymore.

"You're surprised about something here," she suggests. "Something about me."

Not only is the field different from the landscape I pictured, but the cabin smaller and rougher. The woman seems wilder, almost primally uncivilized judging by the look in her eyes, though she speaks directly and with confidence, as if she understands far more about me than I know of her. What is it that seems such a contradiction? Before, everything about her seemed so precisely arranged, like a soft watercolor sketch of a woman obscured by mist. Now I see her clearly, in sharp focus, and realize much of what I guessed I knew about her was my own invention. Even now, all the preconceptions with which I arrived still overlay the reality of the tangible woman before me. The truth is, I know nothing about her.

I don't have to be intimidated. She doesn't know me, either.

"Last time, I did think it was strange," I admit. "Finding you out here." Immediately I second guess what I've said, but decide I need to be less self-conscious. I won't elaborate, or correct myself.

She seems pleased, or at least curious.

"I mean discovering you out here, looking like you do," I can't help elaborating. "It is unusual." I haven't said much, but I'm pleased to find myself able to speak at all.

"Looking like I do?" She turns, reveals herself from another angle, glances down at her own body. It's as if my mention of her appearance, making her aware of my scrutiny, has for the first time made her realize that she possesses a physicality of her own. "Looking like what?"

"Well, not like someone camping out alone in a field." This misses the point I was trying to make. "Clean, attractive and... composed. As if you don't need anything more than you already have."

One arched eyebrow lifts. "I try to exist simply. I try to need only what I already have."

I want to offer more, but know I shouldn't focus so much on her appearance. Still I keep looking at her. I want to know everything. I want to ask why she's out here.

"Here I can escape distraction," she says, seeming to choose words carefully. "My work is difficult to do around other people."

"Work? Working on what?"

"See what I make." She gestures at her home, and turns. "Come inside." Her hand finds a doorknob, swings open a narrow wooden door to reveal a darkness inside. In my memories of this place, all the images replayed in imagination after our first meeting, her little home was a simple triangular facade lacking windows or doors. Of course that's absurd, I realize.

I follow where she leads. The door shuts behind.

Even after my eyes adjust, it's hard to see anything clearly. Side walls slope inward to become ceiling, meeting at a point not far overhead. A single room, lacking bathroom, sink, kitchen. I see no food, no clothing other than what she's wearing. In the center of the floor several rough-textured, unevenly shaped blankets are spread in a pile, one on top of another, various shades of brown and dark green. I imagine this is where she sleeps, between or on top of layers, depending on the temperature at night. On the floor beside the blankets is an unlit pumpkin-colored candle in a hammered silver bowl. The only pieces of furniture are a broad, low table and a small bookshelf beneath the lone window, both rough unvarnished wood. The window is obscured by dust and grime so, like frosted glass, it allows light to pass, but no visible detail.

"Aren't you ever afraid," I ask, "out here alone?"

Her eyes widen in surprise. "Why would I be afraid? Are you afraid now?"

I'm considering how to respond when she turns away, leans over the low table, its surface covered with loose, disordered papers.

"My making." She selects a brown portfolio wrapped many times with homespun twine made of green and black fibers. "Would you like to see?"

She unwinds the cord and the bundle bursts open from the pressure of its contents, dozens of coarsely textured sheets of hand-made paper full of pulp and fiber, seedpods and leaves, and even bits of flower. These varied tints and textures underlie writings in a hand somewhere between cursive and calligraphy. Pen strokes of uneven thickness, from inky wetness to dry scratch. Each page she displays briefly, not long enough for me to read, or even be certain what I'm seeing, before she flips to the next. Indecipherable scrawled lists, paragraphs of reference-like text, all heavily illustrated. Flower blossoms, fish tails, dandelion gone to seed. Wild thistle, darkly outlined and cross-hatched. The words may be English, but my eyes never make any sense of them. The light here is dim, the pages always moving, each turning out of sight before the next is revealed too briefly. Past encyclopedic entries, blocks of text with footnotes and marginalia in different colors. Diagrams, scientific graphs. All so strange, bewildering and yet, whether or not they contain some meaning I'm unable to discern, all undeniably beautiful. Varieties of plant life, sketches of the bones of creatures. A kind of map, topology of land and a tributary structure of streams and rivers, superimposed over a red ink sketch of the ringed cross-section of an ancient tree.

The woman stops turning pages, and though she doesn't close her book, I look away from it, look up at her face instead. I feel I should say something, offer judgment of her art project, or whatever this is. At least I can tell her that it's lovely and amazing, and I'd like to see more, even if I'm not sure I quite understand.

"Now I've let you see my poems." She closes the folio, wraps the twine around.

Poems? I feel like if I want to remain, I ought to comment on what she showed me. Otherwise I have to go. Why can't I think of something to offer? I shoot a glance at the other papers left on the table, loose sheets not bound in folios. These are similar, thickly textured paper covered in letterforms, handwriting that must be hers. Words, drawings, diagrams, recipes. This must be some taxonomy of the living and inert world I'm unable to grasp. One thing I do know, I see her differently now. I want to tell her I had no idea about this, that I only came here because what I thought I knew made me curious.

Then I see on the shelf a number of books, not loose folios like the first but proper bound hardcovers, brown or dark brown leather. I wonder if these books are different in kind, or finished versions of the kind of work-in-progress just shown me.

She returns the folio to the table. "Now you've seen all of me."

I'm certain I've been affected by her revelation, but can't explain how or why. Images echo without comprehension. I want to delve deeper, open myself to knowing more. "I'm not sure I understand."

"Making isn't for understanding." She doesn't seem disappointed in my comment. "Making makes for living."

She steps between me and the table, as if to cut off this line of pursuit, perhaps realizing I'm feeling tempted to intrude further without invitation. I look into her eyes. I should go now, I think, should just say maybe we could see each other sometime in the city, some ordinary place with food and drinks. Excuse myself, but say something first. She's right in front of me, looking at me, as if she reads in my eyes all I'm thinking and understands that I'm torn between departing and asking to see more of her. I don't think she blames me for being stuck. She reaches out a hand as if about to grasp, push or pull me in some direction. She doesn't have to actually touch. Her eyes are all dark, no white. Soothing. I think I might say it, might ask if there's any time we might see each other. Not that I don't like this place, but some neutral place, so she won't feel threatened. Some place with food and drinks, other people. Just say it.

Her hand presses my arm. "Why did you come back?" She reads my eyes, waiting. "Because you remembered me?"

My vision blurs. *Come closer.*

Her eyes are shifting, pale blue, lavender gray. She moves, slips out of focus, back in again, so sharp. Her skin pale, the inside of her mouth living pink, her upper lip full. A hint of scent noticed for the first time brings to mind *Parfum de Nuit*, the shop where I bought incense and candles. I close my eyes. Breathe.

"You came here, why?" she asks. "To find me?"

I don't answer yet, trying to read in her face what I should say. She seems to anticipate my answer. The truth.

Open my eyes.

"Yes. Just to find you."

The door remains shut, the window lightless. The dim gray pervading the room is the same color she wears. It's all I can see, it covers everything. She unfastens the front of her jacket, reaches back and shrugs it off. A series of simple movements and all the other clothing, which before seemed fitted, falls away as if immaterial, no longer needed. Just skin now.

She pulls me down.

It's impossible this is happening, unbelievable that such a raw fantasy, too improbable to admit, is shifting into reality. Her light body, a private wish, a demented fever dream. Now we're moving together. She's revealed to me. I know her, recognize her through all the things she hasn't said. Unexpected things, her fragrance. The smell of skin, soft and private, covered until minutes ago. Not flowery or sweet, but delicate and rich.

Her body and mine, swimming weightless, almost blind. No gravity, no time. Everything in the sensation of touch.

I whisper, "Tell me your name."

She gives no answer.

I see things that don't belong in this room, images I must have brought with me. Flashing eyes watch from outside, above and all around. I focus on her, ignore the rest. There's nobody watching, just us. The only thing real is what's transpiring here. Not before. I wonder what's become of me, where I've gone, then dismiss it all.

"Go light," she says, quiet as breath. "Almost tickle."

The mind has power, to transport and transcend. Even a mind broken as mine can be revived by need.

Closer, deeper, in and out of blissful dreams. Or not dreams exactly, because they remain intact after I'm awake again. I'm confused. How can this be real? I slip loose, try to focus, fail. Am I really here, sharing this place of hers?

Quiet and rest, solitary in sleep, dreaming another river. Then back here again, together, bodies moving. The sizzle of desire, pleasure building to intensity, the urgency of release as if nothing matters but this time, this moment. Activity passes between action, lull and delirium. Always the sharpness again, the taste of salt. So thirsty.

"Now fast," she says.

For too long I've been stuck in wakefulness, dying for sleep. Now I sleep without effort and only barely, briefly pass into clarity before it slips away again. Feel such relief, such perfect relaxation. Nothing external matters, nobody can harm me. Not my boss, not Karl's judgments. Certainly not Michelle. All problems solved, questions answered, worry and self-defeat so easily, finally discarded.

"Force," she says. "Strength."

This woman beside me, I don't exactly know her. This first thing I understand is she's not Michelle. Somehow, I've escaped. I want to know more.

Eyes close, open again. How much later? I don't care about the passage of time. And she's still here, not vanished. The physical persists. This is real. She sprawls naked beside me, not hiding herself. Now watching me. My eyes are hungry in this darkness, starving for any detail. I smell skin, feel the texture of skin, but can barely see. The entire world is nothing but her smooth landscape hidden in darkness, shimmering in and out of existence.

"I still can't grasp this," I hear myself say.

She's sitting up, awake. "That's because it's new."

"How long has it been?"

She gives no answer, tilts her head sideways. Hair perfect black, skin pure white. Eyes invisible.

"How long have I been here?"

For a while she seems to have forgotten my question, or chosen to disregard it. "Not really very long."

We've rushed past preliminaries, from first glance, to acquaintance, then upon third sight to a sudden intimacy. So many steps missed along the way. I want to reset things, render circumstances normal between us. Is that even possible? This morning — or whatever morning that might have been — I left home, hoping for nothing more than to speak to her again. Just to express my interest or attraction would have been enough. Maybe I'm foolish to worry. This might be easier, so many awkward stages skipped. Still I want to backtrack, at least try to relate normally. Pretend to be real people.

Her expression shifts as if responding to my thoughts. It's strange, the way her eyes and mouth are sometimes visible, and express her emotions without words, yet at other moments they're only blank spaces in the dark.

"We crashed together," she says slowly. "That's unusual. Isn't it?"

"It is," I say, still uncertain. "Tell me your name, at least that. We can begin again. Let's start with names." I'm afraid she's going to evade. I've asked before, I'm not even sure how many times, and still don't know.

She appears perfectly untroubled, even amused by my question. "My name is Lily." Her face seems luminous in contrast to her straight black bangs and darkly adorned eyebrows and lips.

"My name is Guy." I extend my hand.

She leans on her left elbow, frees up her right hand for a brief, formal handshake.

What next? We're both exhausted, dreamy, blissful. Also comfortable being naked together, apparently.

"Lily." That's something, a start, but I want more. "Tell me about yourself."

She glances around the confined space, gestures toward her papers and books. "You saw."

"No, the rest of your life."

A pause. "You already know."

"I mean, whatever you do when you're not working here. Where you come from. Your family, job. All that stuff."

She exhales in a way that seems exasperated. "So many questions."

This takes me by surprise, the first hint I've seen of anything but a desire for closeness and perfect acceptance of my every natural impulse.

"I'm not trying to..." I began. "Not trying to demand, just hoping to normalize things between us."

"Normal." She appears puzzled. "What would you say if I told I saw lights in the sky at night?"

"What do you mean? Are you saying that you did, or—"

"What if I said I know a place where time doesn't move?"

I still don't understand. "Do you mean—"

"Would you believe these things because I told them to you? Or do you only believe what you experience yourself? How do you know things? How do you decide which are the things you know, and which you were wrong about?"

I can only guess she's making a point about the meaninglessness of my desire to know more about her. Do we know by seeing, touching, or learn from being told? Is it possible to come into possession of knowledge in other ways? But what does that have to do with us?

"Lily, I don't understand why you're asking me these things."

Her fingertips trace my skin, shoulder to clavicle. She smiles at me. Lily is her name.

My mind slips, relinquishes whatever concerns it might have been trying to contain. I lapse into physical arousal, a sudden onset that washes over everything. We press together, muscles clenching, urgent. Together again, not the first time, not the tenth. This is all surreal, confusing. Where am I? The urgency of my desire, of hers, as if this coming-together might never recur, must be grasped in desperate fear that all the future might vanish.

I know this isn't the last time, not unless I've lost my mind. I know this place, know her.

There's a flash, a brief glimmer of unreality. I wonder if this is really happening after all — am I lying somewhere else imagining this? — but shove this uncertainty aside. We're still together. I know what I feel, can read the feedback she gives. Her hands on me, the sweat and rhythm of her body sprawled, entangling me. Her cries, like an animal lost—

After, Lily is first to speak. "I wonder what you came here wanting?"

She stands, and I think I've never seen her like this since the beginning, naked and upright. I see her better now. The light has changed, or she's allowing me to see. She crosses to the table, picks up loose pages as if she doesn't recognize them.

I remember her question. Does she require an answer? I consider.

She brings back a different book, shows me. "Maybe what you found isn't what you wanted."

Pages decorated with calligraphic symbols, anatomical diagrams of non-human skeletons, angry ink gestures approximating letterforms. This time she lets me linger, doesn't flip past each page too soon. This extra time to look and consider doesn't matter, though. The words are impossible to read. The characters must be foreign, or so small I can't focus in this light. Some of the animal shapes seem familiar, not from anything I can name, but maybe repeated from the other book she showed me before.

"Don't worry," I respond, trying to reassure. "Everything you've shown me is beautiful."

Then I remember where else I've seen some of these designs, shapes and runes. Not here in her books, but outside. Smeared blood on the rocks, lines carved into tree bark. Constructs of bleached bone, mobiles dangling from brown strings resembling dried sinew. These patterns, a common visual language. What does it tell?

She takes back the book, sits with legs crossed, waiting until my eyes return to hers. "Will you stay? Do you have to leave?"

I sense her effort at control, not directing me with words, but exerting nonverbal pressure, power simmering beneath the level of the audible. Also, there's the book which, even after she's drawn it away, seems to echo in my awareness. Contents both long-familiar and frighteningly new, tugging at my desires and what I assume to be my native intention. How long have I been under the sway of her influence?

I glance at the book resting shut in her lap, and want to snatch it back. It doesn't matter that I don't understand what the pages contain. My certainty that it explains something, offers answers to questions I don't yet fully grasp, doesn't depend on my speaking the language. Its contents, expressive art and indecipherable text, entice in the same way as Lily herself. I comprehend, even without understanding. How much certainty is needed to grasp desire? A little mystery is allowed.

Of course there's my usual need to categorize all I encounter, and I do feel uncomfortable, allowing loose ends to spin untethered to anchor points in my mind. How long can I let the unknown and unknowable ricochet around my subconscious, triggering dreams and desires beyond my awareness? I wonder, will I obsess on Lily's pages, the way I was obsessed with the woman herself from the moment I saw her, even before I knew her name, or anything about her art or her body?

"I must have come looking for something," I admit. "You're right, but I'm not sure exactly what it was." I sit up, and realize I've been prone for... How long? Feels like weeks since I've stood up, months since I've been outside. No food or drink, no sunlight, just this room. The two of us lying here together. Lily and me.

That need to categorize and explicate has been part of me much longer. But I'm trying to find a new way to live, different rules. A new map. I need to focus on telling, instead of asking.

Start with myself.

"My roommate, Karl, we're very different. He's tough, and simple, for better and for worse. He says I should be more like him. Lately I've wondered if he's right."

Surprised, Lily laughs, the sound an unexpected brightness. "Try to be Karl?"

I shrug, realizing that's what Karl would do.

"He laughs about my name." I imitate Karl's drawl. "You're the least guy-ish dude I know, Guy."

"I'll make a new name for you." Lily closes her eyes.

This eases me toward sleep.

When I'm awake, I wonder about time again. The barrier between here and there seems thin, almost nonexistent. Sleep is such an effortless thing, it's hard to imagine I ever experienced trouble. When I want it now, I allow it to happen. Together with Lily we pass back and forth. In between, we talk or we move together, bodies shifting from one state to another, an autonomic cycle without striving. With any passing of time, the hunger recurs.

Later I wake to find her kissing my chest, my shoulder. Her lips softer than skin, so impossibly subtle, luminous in the dark. When I shift, she senses I'm awake too. Her eyes smeared darker than blood, shadowed the black of dead coals. Like slashes of warning on a stone face overlooking the river.

I feel no pain.

Into another strange dream, and out again. I open eyes, certain it's over. I'm home again. This never really happened.

But Lily remains beside me. I'm still in her place, have remained so long, I'm sure it must be real.

So quiet. I'm used to trying to sleep on the rolling surface of the Columbia. This river is narrower. The sound of its rushing is faint, maybe inaudible from here. Sometimes I believe I hear water moving, other times I dismiss it as only memory. A different place. Life is always a cycle, absence and recurrence, day and night, sleep and waking, breaking and rebuilding. Loneliness seemed to last forever, but was it really so bad? Now that it's long ago, the pain has shifted, become someone else's burden. Poor bastard.

I watch her sleep, hold my breath watching her breathe. Sometimes her movements are so subtle, I'm afraid her exhalation is nothing but illusion. That she's not really alive here beside me, and only the inevitability of my own respiration convinces me she must possess the same need.

Just as often I come awake to find Lily watching. What else does she do to pass time while I sleep? Sometimes I discover her up, moving around the room. Then she glances over, catches me watching, and I fall away again before I can speak.

Forever night. When we're both awake, connection is inevitable. Bodies always hungry again.

Sometimes she watches me for such a long time, I feel I should offer words. "I feel happy," I tell her.

"What do you think is happening?" Lily asks.

"Everybody wants something," I say. "Some needs, only others can answer."

"You're happy because I gave something you wanted?"

"No, because I finally decided. Then as soon as I acted, I found it. Found you."

She glances away, toward the papers on the table. Her hair falls, a wave of incredible blackness spilling over her shoulder and down her back.

Another sleep.

For the first time in forever, I remember my work. For centuries, nothing has seemed to matter but the two of us, here. But I know if I miss work, Constant will make trouble. Though what I have with Lily seems enough, seems like everything, I know that other world hasn't stopped existing. I still need my job. Have to eat, pay bills.

Though Lily says nothing, her eyes tell me she understands a shift has occurred. She sits up, watches me dress. She listens to me promise I'll be back, assure her that all I want is to be here with her again. As soon as I can. I want her to speak, tell me she understands, but she offers only touch. No words.

"I have to," I say.

Then I'm walking, looking back, too dark to see. I've stayed here all day, into the night. Maybe more than one day. I have no idea what time it is. So much remains unknown, even more than I realized. My old life comes into view again, I can't believe how far away I've been. This world still exists. All I left behind.

The canopy of pines and firs over Cayson's house and driveway seem fake, props set up by some designer trying to ease my transition from one place to another. I find the yellow gate, stare at my car, waiting for all this to snap into clearer awareness. Some indisputable signal to convince me I'm back, this is real. After waking from such a lengthy dream, I find the other world hasn't completely disappeared, still lingers like a fog. Half-drugged, I struggle to remember. Where did the time go?

I don't know what day it is, whether I have to work tomorrow.

But this is my car. Keys are in my pocket. I remember this began with my plan to go fishing, but that's something I never ended up doing. There was the river, and I walked through the trees, found Lily and then—

Fell together, learned her name, and much more. Now I'm here. It seems ridiculous, trying to add up how much time passed. Between intimacy, sleep, and moments of talk, too much to measure. An accumulation of time, sensation and meaning impossible to quantify. Yes, it was better than I could hope. I hold it in the front of my mind, feelings and smells alive and brilliant in memory. I don't care what else happens, what I have to sacrifice. I'll pay any price. I'll go back.

The drive home is tinged with that presence, another world overlaying this one. Sensations so vivid and pleasurable, I question why I'm heading home at all. Remember my car, the road ahead. Try to focus.

Her skin, texture of darkness. Touch of delicate lips and tongue. Lily's sounds, light and deep, the grasping of fingers. An endless loop runs in my head, becomes narrower as I focus on favorite details.

By the time I reach the Columbia River, this world still appears dark, but I can barely tell if that's real. Most of what I see is not my solid surroundings, but her phantom left behind. I may have to go, but of course I also have to return.

# Chapter 13

### Now that I know her name

I've slept all the sleep I'll ever need. Now I'm home, another bed, a different river. Only a few hours until I return to work, but I'm free of my usual worry about what's to come. Whatever I require will come to me. Now that I hold her name, have felt her, known her, slept beside her, everything is changed. Everything.

I remember her name.

*Lily.*

So effortlessly I slip between dreams, one to another and back out again. Alone here, now, I feel her. Even in her absence, I retain this newfound calm.

This is something Michelle could never feel, or even comprehend. With Michelle there were no wild cries, no commingled sweat. Only constant reproach, the droning hum of indifference, the soft violence of unspoken disappointment.

My hunger returns but Lily isn't here. The wanting within me rises, a brand of desire so intense, so vividly present, it is almost painful. Feeling of such potency is undiminished by her absence, but only hides within a mind's inner folds.

*Trying to wake.*

Eyes closed, I see red, imagine blood where none exists. Jagged red smears on gray stone, configurations of shattered bones piled, living heat pulsing within veins. Life spurts from urgent fissures, drips from fevered lips, vacates without warning. A form slumps, grows cold, waiting again.

Where am I?

# Chapter 14

## Speculation on the value of a gift

In the morning, my mind is focused like never before. My surroundings resemble the life I used to live, but the anxiety so long carried is gone. I feel capable of facing anything, unworried by all the burdens that made stress seem a necessary, constant state. A job where I don't fit in, a roommate who expects me to emulate him, even an ex-wife who only chips away at me. Everything remains the way it's always been, but the person at the center is stronger now, more self-assured.

Already since waking, my emotions are ranging all over the place. Excitement, relief, worry. A persistent nagging urge to keep looking out my bedroom window, over and over, to confirm I'm still on the Columbia River and not elsewhere. Sunlight streams through thin curtains, the first daylight seen in forever.

I get up, find Karl's door standing open, his bedroom empty. There's no sign he's been here at all since last time. How long ago was that? I'm accustomed to being unsure how long it's been since Karl last returned home, but now I'm similarly unsure of my own timeline. I don't remember what day it was when I left.

Fed up with Karl's patronizing, and twisted up in envy and frustration amplified by yet another of Michelle's manipulations, I finally gave in to becoming myself. I haven't done as Karl suggested, but something better. Haven't toughened up, or tried to become more mindlessly simple. It's hard to believe I was so upset. Michelle getting remarried takes nothing at all away from me. She's the last person I desire. She possesses nothing at all that I want, except maybe my books.

What I believe led to this change in me, this fresh start, was simply the decision to start over. I bought new music and books, along with tea and some pleasant-smelling things, selected elements intended to form the foundation of a different self. All it took was to hold in mind what I desired, take a few steps toward it, and everything fell into place.

No question, I have to go back to work. I don't know if it's Wednesday, Tuesday or what, whether I missed one day or maybe two. Better if I just shower, get dressed, and go in. Whatever clownish bullshit Constant hits me with, I'll deal with it. He's the boss.

One thing, though, I need to stop driving myself crazy trying to understand Lily. There's no reason she has to tell me everything about herself all at once. A little mystery won't hurt me. A few unanswered questions. Of course I feel a little exposed. That's fine. It's better than where I was before.

Much as I want to return to her immediately, some part of me wants to stay away, to wait until she misses me enough that she's willing to grant more of what I ask. The side of me that doesn't care, that wants to hurry back, is stronger. Whatever Lily's past, however different we might be, she's worth the risk. If I wanted to play things safe, I could find someone like Michelle. Look where that got me. My earlier, more fretful mind keeps speaking up, urging me to stick to what I know. But that fear is poison. I have to be willing to break myself down a bit if I'm ever going to take on a new shape.

All my strange insomniac fantasies drove me to that field, as if I knew Lily was perfectly designed from my imagination. Wild and mysterious, passionate as a force of nature. What is she? Forest witch? Elemental of the trees? Shapeshifting pagan goddess, or succubus built from dreams? I don't care, don't need to know, and refuse to be afraid.

I want more.

This goes beyond personal evolution. Something weird is happening, not just changes in myself. The world outside is shifting. Lily's doing things already, casting spells from her pages, or working occult experiments beyond my understanding. I think maybe her book contains the blueprint of everything that will ever happen. At least all the details of my life, past and future.

All right, that really does sound crazy. I've got to get moving, jump in the shower. None of these details seem real any more. A job, an office. It's all absurd. I can't believe I'm even bothering to pretend. It should be enough just to say, *I get it now, everything's been fake all along. I disbelieve. Now go away.*

Still, I dress for work, drive in, park, go inside. Jeannine and Tammy seem barely to notice my arrival, like I've never been away.

Constant bursts out of his office. The women flinch, duck their heads and won't look at me. I still don't understand what's going on. Constant hurries up to confront me, shouting.

"What the fuck, office girl, just who the fuck do think you are?" Constant shouts, red-faced and bug-eyed, hands trembling.

"Seriously, boss? I..." I think this must be a joke, can't stop myself. I laugh, just briefly, then catch myself.

He's not joking, not at all. He's literally spitting mad. Saliva shoots through gaps in his teeth and streaks his lips and chin. "No show, no call, no explanation? Then you just stroll in here like the cocksucker you are. Then you laugh at me? Just disappear, long as you want? Then just strut on in here and laugh?" Still gesturing wildly, nose reddening until it appears ready to pop, like an overheated thermometer in a cartoon.

"I'm sorry, I—"

"I own this place, you know that? And you're laughing in my face." He stops, breathing hard through his mouth, hanging slack, then licks spittle from his lips.

"I didn't mean to laugh. I thought you were mad about Karl, getting us mixed up."

"Not Karl, dumb ass. You! What do you think, you can just check out, check in, like this is some hotel, except here you get paid? No big deal, huh? You know it's my money that pays your check, right? You think you just pop out, pop in? Fuck you." He hunches over, out of breath, then abruptly returns to his office and slams the door.

Jeannine and Tammy go back to work. I plan to ask them what went down when I was gone, but I'll wait a while. Sometimes I wonder if it bothers them, Constant referring to me as "office girl," as if comparing me to the two of them is the worst insult he can think of. It seems like the definition of a hostile workplace, the kind of thing an HR or payroll professional ought to stop.

I sit by myself, not working, just glaring at the cubicle wall, becoming angrier every minute. There's no way for me to fix this. I want to talk to someone, but I have no allies here, especially with Karl gone. I'm afraid what I might say if Constant confronts me again. Maybe I'm just trying to convince myself it's better if I get out of here for the day, that none of this is my fault.

I log off my computer, push in my chair. "I'm out for the day. Tell Constant he can write me up if he wants." I start for the door.

Part of me wants to stop, ask for a sanity check, but what would be the point? How much time have I missed, really? A day or two, after so many years of showing up, doing a job nobody else knows how to do. But I don't actually care about the answer, can't even guess what day it is. It has no relevance to the world I live in. Also, I know from Karl's example I could miss a lot more time than I have and still not lose my job. Maybe that's what frustrates Constant into acting like a lunatic all the time. The realization he's running an operation out of control. Nobody has any idea what's going on, who's coming in, who's suspended, written up, or what.

Neither Jeannine nor Tammy says a word as I head out, less than five minutes after I arrived.

Briefly I consider going up to the Kalama. Not yet. I spin my tires out of the parking lot, turn onto Marine Drive toward home.

There's still no sign of Karl's truck in the parking lot, of course, so I take his parking spot. The walk down the stairs, gangways and ramps to the dock is so long, almost nobody ever comes to our door. Karl's house is moored at the end, beyond all the other places near shore. The advantage is that beyond my window, there's nothing but open water, nothing between me and the opposite shore.

I'm surprised to find, leaning against our front door, another piece of apparently hand-delivered mail. Not another letter from Michelle. This is a book-sized parcel, brown paper wrapping cross-tied with black and green twine. I pick it up, find no address, just my first name handwritten. I recognize Lily's angular script, embellished with purposefully artful blots and smears of purple-black ink.

I take it inside, hands tingling with excitement, though only hours have passed since I left her. I never mentioned my address, so can't imagine how Lily found this place. And she must have a car, or some other way of getting here. I was at the office such a short time, I can't believe I missed her.

Kneeling on the floor of the living room just inside the door, I start working the twine, which isn't knotted but woven into a pattern almost like a seamless net. Finally I give up, use scissors to cut my way through, then unfold the many-layered paper. Inside the dense and heavy package I find roughly what I expect: a black leather book. It resembles several others I saw in Lily's home, but this leather is much older, worn with decades of age. The binding is snug so the pages aren't loose, but evenly edge-trimmed. The cover, lacking written title, bears only an embossed gold symbol, a square divided diagonally, the left side subsected several more times, resulting in one large triangle on the right, and counter-clockwise to the left, ever-diminishing smaller triangles nested one within the next. A shape split in two, then one half split again, on and on.

This gift excites me, not so much the design, which I don't understand, but what the offering must signify. I've wondered what Lily wants of me, what she intends to happen. Though I still don't know, I feel this gift comprises a kind of promise. More than flattered, I feel seduced, overwhelmed. This removes all question. Any doubt that remained within me is extinguished. I was foolish to allow uncertainty to linger after I finally conquered my earlier weakness.

I carry the book toward my bedroom, and out of habit glance into Karl's room as I pass. There I see something I didn't notice before. On Karl's bed, another heavy old book, worn black leather, very much like the one I just received. Hesitating in his doorway, I look back and forth between the book in my hands and the one like it in Karl's room. I feel certain that if I cross this threshold, someone will immediately become aware I've intruded. Some faceless woman will appear, catch me venturing where I shouldn't go. From a few steps away, I can see that although Karl's book is similar, it's not identical. The cover symbol is different, a serpentine "S" between vertical lines, subscripted and superscripted by small circles like degree symbols, upper-left, upper-right and bottom-center. All this encompassed by a larger circle. Otherwise the book looks like mine, at least from what I can see from the doorway.

I look down again at the book in my hand, confirm that it's different in this way, that there are at least two books here, each slightly distinct from the other. I'm not sure how I might confuse the two, but I'm afraid they'll somehow be mixed up, accidentally swapped if I get them into too-great proximity. For this reason I take mine into my room and leave it on the bed while I go back to Karl's room to examine the second book. I no longer care if I'm discovered intruding.

Within the pages, I find familiar symbols, drawings of leaves, bones, flowers. Lists that could be alien tide tables, or times of sunrise and sunset as might appear in an almanac, but here I recognize no days, times, or dates. The writing is obscure, yet familiarly so. Here I have all the time I desire to scrutinize these writings and drawings, seeking to decipher. The symbology swims like maddening exotic recipes.

I can imagine just one explanation, much as I hate the possibility: Karl returned to the Kalama without me, and met Lily himself.

Maybe this woman he refers to as Sadie is the person I know as Lily. Has he been seeing her all along? The idea sickens me, casts doubt on so much of what truly matters. I remember our first day fishing, when we walked past her field. I asked Karl about the A-frame, and the woman outside. He said no, he hadn't seen anything. Why would he pretend otherwise, if he really did see her there? Maybe he already knew her, before.

I want to take Karl's book and either hide it or destroy it, but of course he would know I'm to blame. Briefly I try to convince myself the two books might be unrelated. That's impossible, just wishful thinking. Lily's work is easy enough to recognize. I know where my book came from. What else might explain the origin of Karl's?

Feelings writhe in my gut like acid snakes. Anger flashes, shifts to wild-eyed jealousy. I feel capable of doing violence. Just finding someone to be with isn't enough. They have to become my own, someone I can keep. Exclusivity is needed. If that's selfish or too possessive, I don't care. Anything I have to share isn't worth keeping.

I retreat to my room, shut the door. What if I decide my book is the only one that's real? I doubt I can convince myself to forget what I've seen. If Karl hadn't left his book out in the open, I'd still be pleased with what I have. Just minutes ago, a thrilling wave of exciting possibility buoyed me. I flip through the pages of my book, trying to recapture from the inscrutable text that initial rush, knowing it's diminished by Karl possessing almost the same thing.

My hunger to see Lily again seems now like some other man's desire, an emotion experienced second hand. I feel nauseated, dejected, supremely foolish. The physical desire is long gone, as if lust and need were never really part of me after all.

What is it that I retain of her, after being so close, body to body? I might have believed some aspect of her lingered, but now I doubt it. Once we're apart, that touch becomes nothing but memory. I felt powerfully energized this morning. Not only happy to have experienced pleasure, to have been wanted. I believed myself to have conquered stubborn old flaws. Now that's gone. The only feeling I have left is a familiar, nagging sense of having lived too long.

# PART 3

# WHATEVER IS

# MADE

# CAN BE UNMADE

# Chapter 15

### Sadie revealed

The front door squeaks open and air moves through the house. Smell of the river and creosote dockways. Karl speaks, a woman responds, both talking as if they don't realize I'm home. I look out from my bedroom, toward the living room. My pulse quickens and sweat prickles my neck. The front door slams shut.

I emerge to meet Karl with a very thin, straight-haired blonde. She's pretty, with a wide, bright red smile. I exhale in relief. Not Lily.

They stop when they see me. Karl's arm is around the blonde's waist, and he swings her around to face me. She's not only narrow-framed, but unusually tall. She's as tall as Karl and me in her heeled pumps. Her abbreviated black leatherette dress is revealing, both below and above, with a plunging slit down the front almost to her navel. She's an attractive woman, though not what I might have guessed. I shouldn't be surprised Karl would be attracted to someone who wears her sexuality on the surface. But she's friendly rather than threatening. Her wide smile is apparently natural, unforced.

"I've been trying to get you to meet," Karl says. "Guy, this is Sadie."

She offers her hand. On the web of skin between thumb and forefinger is a small tattoo, a circled S. It's the symbol from the cover of Karl's book. My mind races backward, trying to recall if I saw any tattoos on Lily's hand.

"Nice to finally meet you," Sadie says.

Her manner conveys an easy directness, enough to make me like her immediately. "You two have been having a lot of fun, lately. Karl's barely been home or at work."

"We've been here plenty, Tiger," Karl says. "You're the one who's always gone."

I'm sure I would've noticed if Lily had any tattoos. There's nothing to worry about. They're two different women, nothing alike. Lily's at least four inches shorter, with a curvier build and dark hair. I try not to smile too obviously as this feeling of relief expands into something near giddiness. My outlook keeps swerving between extremes, from a rock-bottom of hopeless futility, to my amazing coming-together with Lily, then straight home from an awful morning at work, to receive the incredible gift of Lily's book. Then I saw the second book in Karl's room, and came crashing down in another panic. Up and down, back and forth. I'm not even sure now there was a second book. What did I really see? Sadie's tattoo reminds me of the symbol on the cover, but I'm really not sure. Maybe I can get a closer look.

All I know is the important thing: Sadie isn't Lily. Possibilities remain open with Lily.

Karl and Sadie keep looking around, as though maybe they're confused to find me home. Maybe they intended to spend some time alone, or just make a quick stop before getting on their way. I should make clear I don't want to get in their way, but we're still in the middle of this introduction dance. Karl veers Sadie toward his old half-ton convertible sleeper sofa. I sit across from them on the ottoman of the Papasan chair. Karl leans close enough to whisper something in Sadie's ear, then punctuates it with a quick kiss. The delicacy of this surprises me. He pats Sadie's thigh, squeezes possessively where skin emerges from her too-short dress, as if affirming her physicality remains both solid and accessible to him. She sits with knees pressed together, hands in her lap where the dress terminates. I find myself unable to stop looking at Sadie's legs, her feet, all her revealed skin. I realize this might look bad, probably gives the wrong idea. I'm not trying to leer, only confirm whether she's the one I saw that night in Karl's room. Her toenails were painted, and though it was too dark to see color, I imagined the same red as her lips tonight. Maybe this is her color. I'm unclear about everything, including what I actually remember, and which of my own embellishments have intruded upon the realm of memory. All that seems like months ago, already.

"Why not take a picture, Tiger?" Karl seems proud, rather than annoyed, perhaps flattered at my paying attention to Sadie. He turns to her. "Sad Sack here, he's been needing to get himself a woman real bad."

"That was true," I say, trying to be casual.

"I've been meaning to see if Sadie knew anybody for a setup," Karl says.

"Actually, something happened," I add. "A surprise." I want to reveal everything, not only to impress them, but to savor the pleasure of revisiting the experience in the retelling.

But when the words come out, when I tell of meeting someone, stumbling into intimacy, I find myself changing the story. I give a different name entirely, not Lily. I invent broad details, describe someone very different from Lily. I realize the woman I envision is designed to make Michelle jealous, rather than tell any truth about Lily, or even make Karl envious. I don't feel bad for changing the story. It's no disrespect to Lily, but it does bother me, not knowing more about her. I don't even possess enough of her basic information, where she's from, how to reach her. Of course I have to invent. Even after so much occurred between us, there's more she's withholding.

The woman I describe lives just across the Washington side of the river in Vancouver, not in Portland, and not twenty miles north near the Kalama River. It's a nice condo downtown, above a Thai restaurant and an internet cafe with these great organic ginger oatmeal cookies and chai milkshakes. I invent everything in the moment. A woman I'd like to meet, a place I'd be glad to go.

"Ooh, Thai food," Sadie says. "Let's get Thai tonight. Mmm, spicy hot."

"Seriously, girl?" Karl asks.

Sadie nods, excited. "Can we?"

Karl watches me, ignoring Sadie's request. "This all for real, Tiger? I haven't been gone all that long."

"Long enough. Things advanced quickly. I went from no prospects to, I guess, a relationship. Nights together, and plans for more."

"Damn, Tiger." Karl's eyes are wide with disbelief. He runs a hand over his stubbled scalp. "You gone and done it."

I lean closer, craning for another look at Sadie's tattoo.

Karl releases her hand, smacks both palms down on his thighs. "Okay. Thai it is, then."

Sadie rises grinning, clapping fervently, crying, "Woo-hoo!" cheering exuberantly, both arms raised.

"For real, now, Tiger?" Karl shakes his head. "You actually got you a girl."

"What's so hard to believe? You stay away so much, you'll miss a few things."

"Nah, bullshit. You're making up bullshit so I'll quit ragging you." Karl raises an eyebrow as if restraining himself from saying something nasty, for Sadie's sake. "Seriously, all the way, I mean you..." He trails off, the question implied with a forward gesture of his hand.

I don't want to answer, but I'm unsure why. Lily and I slept together in both senses of the phrase, and that's all he's trying to confirm. I set my mouth in a serious expression, and offer an abrupt nod intended as tactful affirmation.

"Well shit, there's my old buddy." Karl turns to Sadie. "Old boy here ran a seriously long-ass dry spell. I tried to give some special Karl-daddy advice. You realize I got the kind of know-how can help any man pitch the woo."

"I don't want to jinx anything," I say, trying not to grimace. "It's too early to be sure how it's going to work out. Anyway, I don't want to keep you two from your plans." I trail off, expecting they'll want to head out for their Thai dinner. Though I'm still curious about some matters, and want to know more about Sadie, I realize I can't ask about it.

Sadie turns to Karl. "Look at him. Guy sure looks like he wants to ask something."

The biggest question I have is about what I saw in Karl's room, but Karl already told me there was no woman. What if I ask, and it was actually some other woman, not Sadie? I don't want to get Karl into trouble he doesn't deserve. Already today with the book I thought I saw in Karl's room, I almost jumped to the wrong conclusion, that it was from Lily. This thought about the book gives me an idea how to get them started talking. I run into my room, expecting my book to be gone, that maybe it never really existed in the first place. But it's still lying there on my bed. I grab it, return to the living room and take the same place on the ottoman.

Karl and Sadie are debating dinner options. It's definitely going to be Thai, but the question remains whether to eat at the restaurant, or get take-out.

As if I'm not interested in what they're saying, I rest the book on my knees and ease it open. The volume is dense as stone, nothing like a construct of paper, ink and leather.

"Guy, you're eating too, right?" Sadie asks.

I pretend I haven't heard. Just keep browsing the pages, waiting for them to notice.

"Yo, Tiger," Karl says.

I look up. Karl has finally seen me flipping the thick leaves of obscure diagrams and nonsensical lists. I'm not really trying to make sense of what I'm reading, merely doing this for show, though I remain convinced the contents of the book must carry hidden significance based on secret intent, which I need only decipher to unlock. Still determined not to speak, I keep my eyes on the pages, waiting for any reaction.

Karl seems irritated, impatient, but betrays no hint of recognizing the book. "What's that for?"

"The woman I mentioned, she's an artist," I say. "She made this for me."

Sadie smiles, bright-eyed, seeming straightforwardly pleased for me, impressed at the romance of the gift. Karl offers his familiar slack-mouthed shrug, conveying zero interest in the book. At least that's the impression he's making, not merely pretending indifference. My book seems genuinely of no more interest to him than any of my other possessions. What can this mean? I'm more anxious than ever to slip into Karl's room, confirm the presence of the second book.

As Karl refocuses attention on the folding yellow menu from Bay of Siam, I return to the open interior of my book, brightly illuminated beneath the standing lamp just over my shoulder. The hundred-watt bulb lights the pages in a way I haven't seen before. The thickest lines of ink glisten black, and the paper's texture is veined, like living skin. This is my first chance to examine the book under good light. The first pages are blank, other than odd symbols like dice in a row that I guess signify dates. Then a title page, larger words comprised of letters that look like Old Norse runes that should be carved on a Viking sword or shield. Some of the characters are almost familiar. A backward "F" with arms pointing up or down. Variations on "T" with the cross-bar peaked or slightly angled. Several jagged, linear versions of "S" or "Z." Most bear no resemblance to any Roman characters I've ever seen. All angles and crude strokes.

Next, a few pages containing mostly blocks of words, structured more like encyclopedia or textbook than narrative. Intermittent illustrations receive greater emphasis than text. On page seven, beneath a spill of words resembling a poem of ecstatic gestures in some exotic tongue is a pseudo-anatomical rendering, like a sculpture in many parts. Interconnected but unrecognizable organs, colored vivid gold and green and dark brown. Page eleven, a structure of bones, some human, others curved and tapered like spears, part of some never-known sea creature. Their color as rendered is darker than the pale white of laboratory skeletal samples, gray dark and heavy as the smooth stones along Lily's river.

All the components seem familiar, product of Lily's hand. I'm not sure what she hopes I'll derive from this. Is it communication? Something I should study until I'm able to read and understand, or a gift of art, to be enjoyed for its obscure poetry? Because it's from her, I want to believe it reinforces our connection, the way in which we fell together, and how quickly we both transformed. Though I worried that we parted in argument, under a cloud of disagreement, or at least that my need to leave disappointed her, her gift of the book reinforces that we're not finished. I still intend to return, always have.

"So, Tiger, I'll run for dinner, that place on Hayden Island, and come right back. You want the usual Pad Kee Mao, five stars, with tofu?"

"No, I don't need to intrude into your plans," I insist. "You should have your private dinner, whatever you had planned."

"Got no plans, so I'm bringing your usual, dummy, plus whatever my spicy lady here wants. For me it's Salmon Red Curry, four stars, and maybe to split, a Hot Basil Fried Rice."

Sadie decides on number fourteen, some vegetable stir fry with chicken, three stars. I continue protesting until Karl stops listening. He really doesn't seem to mind the idea of me butting into their dinner plans. I feel ridiculously grateful, almost emotional at the prospect of spending time with them. It's been several weeks since I've shared a meal with anybody.

"A gift like this carries intention." Sadie says, referring to the book I still hold. "A girl makes you something like that, it's special. She made this thinking of you. She put both of you inside it."

Karl stands, pulls car keys from his pocket. "It's got pictures, at least. Not that I have any idea what the fuck's going on there, no offense."

"It means she's not interested in just any man," Sadie insists. "Guy is her focus."

"If I got a book like that..." Karl moves to the door, pauses with his hand on the knob. "...I'd go pick up Thai for my roomie and best girl."

"Sure you don't want me to go with?" Sadie asks.

"Nah. You entertain the old man." Karl slips out.

I feel strange, discussing with Sadie this gift which feels bound up in the intimacy I shared with Lily. I get up, head toward my bedroom, intending to stash the book. On my way I shoot a glance into Karl's room, specifically looking for the book I found on his bed earlier. Now there's nothing on the bed, or the headboard shelf, other than Karl's usual dog-eared motivational and self-help paperbacks. None of these remotely resemble the book I saw, or thought I saw. Karl never went in his room after they came home. Sadie slipped away to the bathroom. I guess she could've gone in there, seen the book and hidden it. Why would she?

I slip my book under my mattress, and arrange bedding to hang over the gap. Now it's hidden, safe.

When I return, Sadie picks up where we left off. "Women give important gifts to men who give us their most intimate selves. It's like a trade."

I'm not sure what to say. Part of me would love to talk more about Lily, but I'm not sure I remember all the details I invented the first time I described her. "She's amazing, but so completely unlike me."

"Karl says you're completely unlike everybody." Sadie giggles with disarming sweetness. "But the same's true of Karl, I guess."

"We fell together in this incredible way, like a dream, and remained like that a long time. But when I left, I was frustrated. I expected to learn more about her. Maybe it was too soon."

"She was already revealing herself," Sadie states with firmness. "Also, that's why she gave you what she did."

"I know it's unreasonable. I haven't known her long enough to demand too much."

"A little unreasonable," Sadie says gently. "When someone gives you a lot very quickly, you shouldn't demand more, more."

I believe she's right, but part of me remains frustrated she won't reinforce my sense that I have a right to ask more of Lily. Maybe next time I see her, I'll back off a little, but still I feel I had a right to expect an answer or two.

"Don't worry, we all do it." Sadie's grin flashes bright, friendly and non-judgmental. "There's no formula for how things should proceed. You plow ahead, hoping you'll get what you want, but sometimes the other person resists, so you just let up a bit. Karl and I had a little of that, at first."

It's a relief, being let off the hook. I should let it go, relax, just be friendly. But I can't help it, can't stop myself blurting out what's running through my mind. "I heard you screaming, with Karl," I insist. "A sound like a wild animal, all night."

Sadie looks down, smooths the hem of her dress over her thighs. "Karl said there was a night, I was away, you thought you heard sounds. Him with someone. A woman."

"You must've been here. It was you."

"No." Sadie doesn't look happy, shakes her head a tiny bit, jaw set.

"I got up, Karl's bedroom door was open. You were sitting on the edge of his bed."

"Why do you think it was me?"

"You were alone, naked in the dark. Why was Karl gone?"

"That never happened." Sadie's hands slide down her thighs, clutch her knees. She appears to be weighing the possibilities, argument or anger. When she looks up, her face is neutral. "You don't get to tell me I was here. I wasn't."

"I'm not trying to get Karl in trouble. I'm not saying he was with another woman. It was you."

"No, Tiger," Sadie says, imitating Karl's drawl.

"Then what," I ask. "What did I see?"

Sadie doesn't appear upset with me, and I'm hoping she doesn't hold anything against Karl because of what I've suggested. I hate having dampened her bright smile and easy nature.

"There's no way to know," I say, trying to make her feel better. "I think sometimes I confuse dreams with real things."

Neither of us speaks again until Karl returns with a paper bag full of Styrofoam containers. We eat in front of the TV, watching the last half of *Caddyshack,* and drinking bottles of Hop Karate IPA Karl brought home.

The movie's almost over, at the scene where the priest blames God for his perfect golf round being ruined by gale winds, rain and booming lightning. Karl stands, yawning. Sadie gets up, follows him to the bedroom. The door clicks shut.

A lot has changed since the night I heard Sadie. Why does tonight blur together with that other time?

I mute the movie, but this makes me feel self-conscious so I turn off the TV and go to my room. What sounds I can't help hearing are different, much quieter than before. Bits of words, muffled laughter. No howls. No screams.

# Chapter 16

### The role of delusion in the remaking of selves

I'm motionless, alone here, stuck between unbearable history and the possibility of a better future no less terrifying. Days spent living within the book, trying to intuit significance from sketched shapes, colors, textures. The more I absorb, the more I believe that, on some level beyond the explicable, I understand. Comprehension can be intuitive or poetic, rather than concrete. Maybe in time, more will clarify, become solid.

I should return to Lily. What's stopping me? I'm afraid if I go back, I'll find her gone.

The front door deadbolt unlocks with a click. Hinges squeak. The sound of Karl arriving home.

I close my book, try to stand and nearly fall, my knees and back stiff from too long lying inert. I listen, wondering if it's Karl alone, or Sadie too. As I venture out, Karl approaches our connecting hall, alone. He clutches a paper bag shaped like a bottle.

"No Sadie?" I ask.

"She suggested you and me ought to hang out a while."

Despite having wished Karl would come home, I'm unsure how this prospect makes me feel. "You don't have to worry about me. I'm fine." I remain within my doorway.

"Sadie can't stop saying how you're this so-great guy. Also, with me being gone so much, it's probably time you and me have a boys' night."

"She's not coming?" Was she put off by the things I said while Karl was getting take-out Thai? Maybe she wants Karl to set me straight. It's possible it's no more complicated than what Karl suggests, just a night to sit around drinking, talking like we used to.

"I think we can survive one night away from our women, Tiger." Karl shrugs, and there's something off about the gesture, like an imitation of Karl performed by someone who barely knows him. An imposter, told Karl often shrugs, seeking to imitate the maneuver but failing to capture the grinning, loose-shouldered impertinence of my actual roommate. This isn't Karl at all. This thought arises out of certainty Sadie is making him do this, a submissiveness so out of character. Then the idea evolves. It's not even him. Maybe I haven't seen the real Karl in a while. This man is so far removed from the person I've known, they don't appear to share any common traits. This one doubts. He hesitates.

From the paper bag, Karl slides a fifth of Johnnie Walker whisky. He holds it up as if uncertain how I might react.

I grin, relieved. "Planning to share?" This is what I need to help me forget. To shut off my mind.

"Believe that. Good and smoky."

I go to the kitchen for two glasses, one with ice for Karl.

"Anything exciting at work?" Karl asks, fake casual, holding something back.

I try to read him. Clearly he's got some kind of story he wants to tell. "You've been gone a long time."

Karl takes his glass, counts ice cubes, seems satisfied. "Well. Constant has me working a special project. Out on the road."

I pour two fingers each, thinking already we both know this tale is a lie. Maybe he thinks I'm fooled. He launches into an overly detailed story, describes every conversation with Constant leading up to Karl being sent out to Astoria, a little town way down the Columbia, on the Oregon side, where it meets the Pacific a hundred miles down. He calls it a reconnaissance trip, says Constant intended Karl to spy on competitors there and in Gearhart, then across the bridge in Ilwaco and Long Beach, Washington.

Numerous details prove he's lying, especially compared to what I already know. Constant's open expression of anger in the office, and open, loud talk about firing Karl. His discussions with Jeannine and Tammy about written warnings and documentations of malfeasance already existent in Karl's personnel file. Especially Constant asking Tammy whether an offer of the yard superintendent job, currently Karl's position, might be enough to lure Tammy's son-in-law back from Christiansen Shipworks. Constant isn't a good enough liar that his frustration and anger could possibly be an act. All this background only clarifies the flaws in Karl's over-embellished tale.

Karl's an entertaining liar, so I let him continue. He describes every detail of meeting, in the Safeway parking lot on his way into Astoria, this shipwright Joe something. Karl claims this old guy Joe used to work at Constant's, and immediately fed Karl all the intel he needed, so Karl and Sadie never actually had to leave the hotel room to figure out everything that was happening with shipbuilding, repair and salvage in that whole region. He and Sadie could just hole up, having fun and getting paid. Karl shows real delight in the telling.

I figure if a storyteller seems to believe and enjoy it themselves, this goes most of the way to convincing the listener. I almost start to consider the possibility Karl's confabulation might possibly be true, that Constant might actually send Karl for nearly a week in Astoria, a little town where within twenty-five miles in every direction there can't be three actual competitors to Constant's operation. Even if he did send Karl, would he put him up in a nice hotel with his girlfriend, and let him run wild on room service? Of course not, and if he did, he wouldn't have been ranting all week about Karl's absence. So clearly I see Karl's deception, yet he goes on spinning, believing he's got me fooled. I wonder how many times I've done the same, offered some version of events, but deceiving nobody but myself?

"This amazing old hotel, restored, refurbished..." Karl trails off. "What do they call that? Anyway, some ancient place from like a hundred years ago, right in the middle of town, across from where they do that Sunday market. All the hipster art kids and sorry-ass beach drunks."

"That's the Elliott." I don't mention the reason I know this, which is that Michelle enjoyed visiting there at least once every year. If Karl finds out I've been to Astoria and the Elliott hotel at least thirty times, it'll put a damper on this whopper of his.

He gulps deeply from the Johnnie. "Yeah, we stayed overnight, I mean, bunch of nights, like four. No, six. Super nice room, like, shit, the nicest bed I've ever slept in. I need to get me a bed like that. Sadie loved that fucker like you wouldn't believe, not just the mattress part. On top there's this super plush comforter, maybe a foot thick. Goose down I think it was." Karl holds his hands out, palms separated by a gap of at least eighteen inches, presumably demonstrating the thickness of this incredible bedding. "Felt like we were buried under feathers six feet deep. You can't hear the outside world through it. Shit, we barely left that bed for two minutes all week."

I finish my whisky, go to the kitchen and retrieve the bottle. "So. Constant really sent you to Astoria for work?"

"Man, would you believe once we settled into that place, with two bottles of this here brown party liquor and a case of this red wine Sadie picked up, we never opened that door again but for room service food?"

"Since when are you a wine drinker?" I enjoy wine myself, but I've heard Karl's enthusiastic disparagement of the stuff so many dozens of times, I never considered having a bottle in the house.

Karl pauses, eyes wide, as if I've seized upon a crucial flaw in his tale which requires him to scramble for explanation. "I drink what Sadie likes, Tiger. That's all. Keep your woman happy, things are easier. Lethe Hills Vineyard, that's what it is." His face relaxes, and he offers his glass, jingling the lone remaining ice cube while he loudly chews the rest. "Speaking of drinks, hook me up here. I don't give a shit about ice. So, what about this woman of yours?"

I mistrust Karl's curiosity about my situation. Usually he only wants to talk about me when he senses a weakness he might pin down and exploit for amusement. "You mean Michelle?" Despite his pretense of sincere interest, I can't imagine he actually wants to hear me describe the stumbling path that ended in me meeting Lily, or whatever name I substituted when I described her before. Or if he does, he'll only want to hear the pornographic details.

"No, dummy." Karl looks at his watch, then at me. "This new lady, what did you say she was called?"

I consider telling him everything. Lily's real name, the true story on the river near Cayson's. I hesitate.

"You damn fucking pussy, I knew it. I knew it! There's nobody. You made up all that shit."

"I did meet someone." I study him, trying to gauge what I can say. It's time to reveal at last a few pieces of truth. "I just don't want to jinx things, acting like I own her. Nothing's really solid or definite. Certain details remain, ah, up in the air."

"Yeah, I mean, duh. We're talking about girls, right?"

I shake my head, look down in my drink. "Karl, sometimes I think you don't like women much."

"Sure, some I don't. I like some, dislike others. That's how it ought to be, both men or women. They're all different. I don't feel the same way about every single woman."

"I know they're important to you from one angle. In the six months I've lived here, you've been with how many?"

"It's been more like a year, dummy. Anyway, we're not talking about fucking. We're talking about the other stuff."

I feel the whisky in my head, fumes rising from my belly, my throat. "That stuff, that's the tricky part. Sex happened easily with her. It's the relationship side I'm concerned about. I admit, I'm worrying a little. Then I thought maybe the book meant something, especially after what Sadie said." I sip again, lean back.

"What?" Karl looks confused. "What book are we talking about?"

"The book she made." I try to read him, looking for deceit. "I showed you. Sadie said it had to be important, a woman giving a gift like that. Something she created from—"

"Whatever you say, man." Karl shakes his head dismissively, looking like himself again. "Must have been another of your boring-ass stories, because I got no memory here whatsoever."

I almost stand, go to my room and retrieve the book, but restrain myself. I'm not sure I believe he actually doesn't remember. Maybe for some reason he's just pretending there's no book, that I haven't shown it to him, that he doesn't have a nearly identical book of his own. Could be he's playing dumb because he wants another look, wants to compare mine to his.

"You saw it." That's all I say.

"Whatever, dude. Anyway, you know, I'm not about tagging maximum ass any more. I'm changing a bit, maybe growing up. Settling down, in a good way. Anyway, maybe we both finally have a shot at outgrowing these traits that hold one back."

This last phrase seems so out of character, I almost laugh. Like some line he's been rehearsing, words he heard in a movie and kept repeating until he internalized them. "Outgrowing traits that hold one back. I hope I am." That's all I can say. "Outgrowing traits."

Karl rubs his mouth with his knuckles. "God damn, this is hitting me. I never had any lunch. Is there something I can eat on, so this whisky don't do me in?" Now he not only looks like Karl, but sounds like himself. He stands, goes to the kitchen and comes back with a box of rye crackers I know are old and stale.

"Let me tell you something she wrote." I blurt this out, without having decided to reveal this.

"What, from this book?"

While I refill my drink, I consider where I want this to go. "No, not that. Michelle. This letter she left."

"Aww, shit no, Tiger. We are not going to talk about how bad you miss your fucking ex. Not tonight."

"Not that. I want to know what you think of an accusation she made." From memory, I summarize the only part of Michelle's letter not centered on herself, about me compartmentalizing everyone.

"Yeah, she's right there," Karl says. "You know I hate the bitch, but she's pretty much dead on."

I feel anger rise, and try to convince myself he simply misunderstood. "She says I need to feel in control of others, psychoanalyze people and put them in slots. Then I'm no longer dealing with actual people who think for themselves, only interacting with collections of traits. Then if a person acts outside my expectation, I freak out and insist they're being insane."

"I don't want to piss you off, but you do that, especially at work. Think you've got everyone nailed down."

I want to keep explaining, try another angle, but give up. "I thought you might say she's wrong."

"It's all right, Tiger. You're a good boy. It's just like you skipped the last stage of growing up. Most guys in their teens, early twenties, life thickens their skin. They get dumped by girls, fired from jobs, crash a car, go bankrupt. But you glued yourself to your first girl and married her. You two built this, sorry, but this mind-fuckingly boring suburban existence. You never actually lived yet."

I want to say he's wrong. I don't have any solution in mind, if he's right. "I'm almost fifty. I don't think I can—"

"You can, Tiger. You just got to break habits."

"Maybe. At least now, I have possibilities that weren't on my radar a week ago, or a month." I stop, unsure how long it's been. My whole timeline, meeting Lily, Karl's absence, hearing Sadie, trouble at work. Everything's scrambled, disordered. I not only have trouble with time gaps, but also sorting events into the right sequence. Maybe it's just the whisky, making it seem worse.

Karl alternates bites of Rye Krisp with sips of the Johnnie. "You won't ever be right until you face up about your ex. That shit was unreasonable, but you keep acting like she's pure good."

"I know. Why did I accept it?" I surprise myself, saying this without equivocation, without offering excuses for Michelle. "Sometimes I tried to speak up, I might sit her down, say we need to talk. But nothing ever changed. She was nicer to strangers than to me. Sometimes she was cruel. I should have been the one to end things, but I didn't. So why do I see Michelle as this ideal partner, someone I should want back?"

"Because she said go, not you. That simple."

"She's the only woman I've known. One person, my whole life. Losing her, it's like I've lost everything. In college, at U of O, it was all Michelle. Things weren't bad then. Junior year, she got pregnant, so we moved back to Portland. Her parents had a guest house over their garage. We got married in the back yard under this huge tree. We recited poems, one of Michelle's, one each by Keats and Rumi. Can you believe someone barely twenty putting her own poetry in a mix with these towering geniuses?" I shifted from the ottoman back to the Papasan itself. "Anyway, we painted everything, all this cliché baby decor, even bought a crib. Then she miscarried. We'd already quit school, gotten married, so we didn't consider going back to Eugene. But there was no baby."

"Sorry, that's tough."

"No, don't be sorry. I'm glad there's no kid. But this offspring who wasn't, this absence where we expected a person to be, that's the reason my life went this direction. I started this direction, got into a flow and just drifted along. I never ran around in college, never went to parties, or tried to meet girls. Michelle and I had friends like ourselves, all married too young. They started having kids, and drifted away. Then it was just us."

"Did you want out?"

"No. I didn't marry Michelle only because she was pregnant. Well, maybe, but I did love her. She was attractive, very smart and confident. Just smashed obstacles out of the way. I remember when she wanted to make me happy, at first."

"Yeah, until she didn't." Karl yawns, stretches, looks inside the empty Rye Krisp box and tosses it aside. "If you look at everything, all the life you missed out on, plus the divorce shitstorm, it wasn't worth it. Right?"

I pause, not trying to be dramatic, but actually pondering his question. I don't know the answer, so I don't respond. Of course I realize he'll take silence as my answer.

"You said she cheated," Karl says with surprising delicacy.

I lean forward, refill my glass, lean back. I can't answer yet, so I lean forward again, offer the bottle to Karl. He extends his glass, I pour him full. Try again.

"Yeah, with a coworker. Not just sex." I gesture, summoning clouds. "Romance, passion. I wanted to believe it had only been one time, so I forgave. Later, I realized she'd never asked for forgiveness. Never promised it was over. I was trying to show I could rise above it."

"Weren't you pissed?"

"I was. I am. But sometimes I miss her so much, it feels like fresh grief. I remind myself why I wanted to stop missing her. Why I should. Now, lately, I have a chance to start over. I believed I'd stop thinking about Michelle as soon as I found sex, a relationship, even go on a date. Now I wonder, but at least I see Michelle as she really is. This new one helps me, this new woman. Still I find myself thinking of Michelle, and feel disgusted about that. I hate my weakness."

"It's not weak, just to think about her. It's only weak if you give up. Man, don't let it keep you stuck."

"That's why this is so bad. I'd take her back, if she asked me. I'd go, even after everything."

"Damn." Karl drinks deeper than he has since the first, then takes another mouthful and holds the Scotch in his mouth. He focuses on me with solemnity. "You know what you need to do? Tell me the most brutal part, all the details, whatever's your worst memory. How you found out, or when she told you to go."

I'm weighing the possibility he suggests. Whether it's reasonable to tell. Whether it might help. Whether I can even do it.

"When you give me the story," Karl elaborates, "you have to tell how it really was. I mean relive it, like put yourself back into the worst pain. Man, that was your wife. She ended your marriage. It wasn't a misunderstanding that she's going to come back and fix. She wanted you the fuck out of her life, out of her house. So when you're telling it, remember. Really make yourself feel how it was."

I don't speak at first, not because I'm unwilling to tell. It's just hard to figure out where in the stream of events to begin. I could set the background for context, why she was stressed, how we'd argued and I'd said something I wished I hadn't. None of that matters.

"It was an ordinary evening. Michelle was standing in the kitchen, boiling linguini and slicing brown mushrooms. There was a giant Costco jug of olive oil on the counter, and a bottle of very pale yellow-green Pinot Grigio, something local. I can picture the color but don't remember the name. I asked what she's making and she looked at me, didn't speak. I can see this sullen face, loose, drooping skin, like a stranger wearing a Michelle mask that doesn't quite fit. Dark bags under her eyes, pain inside welling up like sickness. Or so much poison, it's killing her. I recognized the look. When she finally did speak, her voice was rough. Not just something raw in her throat, but trembling, and loss of control from emotion. Fear and anger, which I didn't understand. It scared me. That's when I realized she'd been crying, alone in the kitchen, making food for herself, but not for me. My first reaction was to back away, tell her I didn't need any food."

Karl leans back, eyes closed. "How'd she say it? Did she blurt it out, or did you have to pull it out of her?"

"She forgot about her pasta, just stirred it robotically for a long time, glancing between me and the boiling water. Like she was about to speak, but her mouth couldn't form the words. She'd start, then stammer, repeat herself, not really going anywhere. She kept apologizing, touching her face. This wasn't Michelle. I started guessing at what she meant to say, making suggestions so she could nod or shake her head. Something about this made me sick. We were only making it worse. Finally I turned away to sit, to wait for her to talk to me, and as soon as I faced away, as soon as eye contact broke, she said the words. 'I don't want us to be together, Guy.'"

"Did you try to argue her out of it?"

"She never said anything important like this unless she'd already been thinking about it a long time. And once she said the words, I knew her mind would never change. So I said nothing. Just sat there, trying to compute, looking at the floor. My mind spun with all these possibilities. Thinking about stupid things like furniture, and bills. Details of a life that was already dead." I stop, refill both glasses, trying to relive what happened next. What really did happen, and what did I imagine later? Breathe deep. "Finally I said, 'Where will you go? I don't get how this works.'"

"You thought she was gonna leave."

"She looked at me confused, said, 'Where will I go?' I said, 'Your income won't pay for another house. Are you moving in with someone else?' She stopped stirring linguini, turned off the stove, and set down the wood spoon. Came over to me, with this softness in her eyes, for the first time looking at me with this gentle pity. She touched my hand, so delicately. I thought, she's relenting, she already realizes she's been all wrong about this. Something changed her mind. Even if it's only that she hasn't considered the financial aspect, if she only wants to stay because she can't afford to leave, that's fine. Good enough. Either way, I'm sure she doesn't mean it. The change won't really happen."

Karl shakes his head, waiting. He knows the outline of my story.

"The next thing Michelle said, she let me know how foolish I was, still am. She said, 'I'm not leaving, Guy. You're leaving. I can't have you here in this house any more. Not another day.'"

"So you were paying most of the bills but—"

"Yeah." I nod. "She set out all the luggage, two pieces of hers and two of mine, and said I should pack my things right now. From the garage she brought in two empty cardboard boxes, not nearly enough for everything of mine. Then she changed her mind, said instead of watching me pack, she'd allow me to do this alone. She said she'd be back in an hour and left the house. I was stunned, just standing there looking around. Thinking I should've said this or that. I didn't become angry. Not at her. I had this weird, chivalrous impulse. Fine, if she doesn't want me, I won't ask for anything. I'll handle it so well, be so strong and noble, this will clarify for Michelle how wrong she's been. I'll leave behind most of what I care about, and when she sees, she'll feel ashamed. Books half mine, music mostly mine, even the beautiful Linn stereo I bought twenty years ago. All left behind. I keep thinking, Michelle seeing all my things, that will guarantee my return to this house. She'll realize our lives are of a single piece. I boxed up my computer, a few things from my desk, just filled one of the boxes. I remember thinking I might be about to cry, and I couldn't do that in case she came back. I left in a hurry, four suitcases, one cardboard box. Does that make sense?"

Karl set the empty glass beside himself on the sofa cushion. "Hell no."

"I mean, do you understand my idea that by taking it well, I kept alive the possibility she might change her mind? The marriage might be out of joint, but not dead. Her declaration might be revocable."

"But you did that for her, not yourself. You wanted to lay on a guilt trip by walking away from things you wanted. Like, fine, I'll leave, but I'll force you to feel bad. You left thinking she'd have to call you back. But did she?"

My eyes burn so I squeeze the bridge of my nose. Not tears, just fatigue. Fumes from my glass. "Of course not."

"You made a mistake. You played it, thinking she'd have to take pity."

I shake my head. "I was just reeling, faced with trying to divide up books and CDs. I couldn't deal with it."

"Whatever," Karl says, seeming to dismiss my suggestion. "I'm saying your old-fashioned gentlemanly approach was bullshit. 'Not at all dear, quite all right.' You thought she wouldn't take you up on it, but she sure as hell did. Too bad, but you didn't mean what you said. Don't say something's fine if it isn't. Don't walk away from most of what's yours, including a four hundred thousand dollar house, saying you don't mind. That's not being a quality person. It's being a sucker."

"Yeah."

"And how'd that work for you?"

"Not too well."

"So you take a few suitcases and that sissy iMac in a cardboard box, and everything else, you let her keep. That big gesture got you shit."

"It's all gestures." I motion widely, implying everything. "Acting."

"You lost me."

"Everybody's got it within them to do anything, good or bad. But we decide how we want to be, and try to play the part. It's only the acting that gives us any hope of being better than the worst parts of ourselves."

"You think?" Karl holds up the Scotch bottle, eyeballs what remains, pours half for himself, and hands me the bottle. "What's the worst you've ever done? Truth. Man, I've done some heinous shit."

The diagonal Johnnie Walker label makes me feel off-kilter. I pour most of the remainder into my glass. "I haven't thought about this in a long time," I begin, without stopping to think. "At a certain age, this neighbor sort of molested me. I don't know, how old is second grade. Eight?"

"Wait, what?" Karl scrutinizes me, squints as if having trouble focusing. "How old was this other guy?"

"I don't know. Older than me, but not adult. Maybe twelve or thirteen."

Karl whistles a descending note. "Fuck, man. How does that make you feel? You want to kill him?"

I shake my head, trying to blink away the surge of feelings coming over me. "I never felt like it harmed me, exactly. I'm not saying I liked any of it. Really everything just seemed like... pointless things to do. I was a kid. It wasn't traumatizing, like rape. He didn't fuck me, anything like that. He'd say if I'd lay down beside him in his bed for a few minutes, he'd give me certain comic books he knew I wanted. And I'd think about whether I wanted the comic books enough to be willing to do whatever it was, and I'd either do it or say no. What he was asking wasn't the hardcore stuff you're probably imagining. I'm not even sure what he was doing, probably just beating himself off with a little naked kid next to him. He didn't touch me, really. The decisions seemed simple. I felt weird after, sure as hell never told anybody, but I didn't worry over it, either. It only happened a few times. He moved away."

Karl makes a farting noise with his mouth. "That's why your sexuality's all deformed and shit, you realize."

"Fuck you, Karl. You want any more of this?" It's an effort, sitting up, focusing on the whisky.

"Nah, Tiger, just kidding. Yeah, go ahead and pour me. Thing is, I asked what's the worst thing you've done. That story, shit. You were a little kid. That dude victimized you. That's not anything you did wrong."

"Yeah," I say, though the suggestion surprises me, until I think about it. "I didn't exactly mean it was my fault. But when you asked, that's what came to mind."

"Dude probably hates himself now. If not, he fucking should. Man, I could tell a whole list of horrible shit. You ready to hear mine, some of the worst, something I actually did?"

I hesitate, put off by this lead-in. "I guess so."

"Man." Karl blows through pursed lips. "This wasn't quite as young as what you said, but similar. Perverted kids, that kind of shit."

"You're serious?"

"Fuck yeah, serious. I messed with my cousin Laurie one summer, a few times. Like first, got her to show me herself. Then look at me naked, touch it. Later, she let me kind of roll around on top of her, not fucking, but you know, sort of sexual. I started touching her, fingering. I thought she liked it, but I don't know now. Shit. I was thirteen, she was eleven, almost twelve. I wanted to act out things I saw in magazines. Tried to put it in her mouth, you know. At least got her to sort of kiss it. Fuck, who knows what I thought I was doing."

My reflex is to tell him not to worry, that he was too young, but I stop myself. It's better if he continues feeling it was wrong. He should wish he could take it back, even if he can't. "So we both admitted these buried stories, revealed our secret shame, or whatever." I wipe my mouth, realize my vision is blurry. "Fucking whisky. But the difference is, your story's about doing something to somebody else. Mine's about being done to."

Karl appears to weigh the distinction, or maybe he's just drunk too. His head lolls sideways, eyes squeezed shut. "You're doing it again, Tiger. Head-shrinking, even liquored up. Anyway, I got to get a little sleep." Both knees pop when he stands, and he lists to one side as if he might fall.

"Yeah, I should too." Now I'm the one lying. No way I can sleep.

Karl staggers a few steps, stops, turns back. "Wait, did I tell you about Constant? This work thing, Constant's big plan?"

I try to remember. "You said something about Astoria."

"Yeah, that's the start of it. Something new for me. Constant's grooming me for management. Man, you watch and see."

"Management?" I ask. "You already supervise most of the guys that work there."

"Management, not supervisor," Karl says, extending his earlier lie. "I wear a hardhat, one of the good old boys. But you'll see. No more welding and shit for me. Constant sees me in a necktie, talking to customers, making deals. Like a boss."

Bad enough Karl believes his employment remains stable, he wants me to believe he has a future in upper management, at a company that doesn't even have upper management. The only person playing the role Karl envisions is Constant himself. This is nothing but wishful thinking, so detached from reality I doubt even Karl himself believes it possible. Maybe that's why we drink, to let our lies become reality, at least for a while.

But I don't tell Karl this. We say good night. I head into my own room, shut my door.

Now that Michelle's back on my mind, I doubt I'll be sleeping. Lily helped me past this, before. Where's Lily now? Too much to think about. I wish I'd never started thinking again.

# Chapter 17

## Weightless in a bed of self-deceit

Just try to rest, that's all. Close your eyes. Lie still.

I see myself from outside, a body sleeping beneath the stars, in a field of grass near a river.

Then I'm back inside my body. Someone's sitting on my chest, pressing down, hands on my face. I struggle to pry the hands away. Fingers part enough that I can recognize that smile. The wide crescent of Sadie's mouth.

The ground softens beneath me. I sink in. The weight holding me isn't heavy, but persistent. Even as she forces me down, her smile remains. I'm halfway under, like floating in cool water, but the ground is silent and dry.

Her skin slides over mine, slippery as if her body is oiled. Even in this moment of fear the sensation is pleasurable in the exaggerated way of dreams, a feeling intense and electric. I want to enjoy it, savor it. The realization that I'm slipping under allows me to simply feel the pleasure, without any thought of Lily or Karl or Michelle or anyone. Nothing matters but the sensation of skin slipping against skin. The longer I accept this, focus on the touch instead of fighting back, the more I'm pushed under. The ground keeps rising. I'm almost beneath the surface.

Sadie stands, moves away, still smiling. Knowing.

The air touches me where now her skin is absent. I want to rise, but the river forces me to listen, the whisper of water's constant need. Memories an endless stream, events which someday I should organize. Occurrences sorted into sequence. Isn't that how time works?

It's important not to confuse one woman with another. When did we meet? I met her in mind, first, saw myself encountering her a thousand times, dreamed coming together, floating past obstacles. I remember women, I've seen faces in crowds. I came to understand the type I wanted, the way she should smell, the acceptance in her eyes. Dark hair, skin pale and sometimes patterned. Her own smell. The taste, a mouth full of blood.

A human suit made of—

Women's faces distinct, each body unique. Don't confuse one with other.

Michelle, lips an unwavering line. Uncompromising in the business of control, never doubting.

Sadie, an outline in darkness. A collection of absent details, defined as indefinite.

Lily, built from dreams. My problem is that dreams are never solid as flesh.

No wonder I can never sleep. These are separate names, shapes, bodies, smells, tastes. Remember the need to understand the mark of each.

Fear shapes desire, the gravity of nearing threat. I'm drawn in, perceiving more than I know, accumulating details. People never met, only imagined. Not physical, but still real. I know them all.

I can accept being under a spell, just have to remember what's true. I realize I'm caught. Knowing helps.

# Chapter 18

## What she gives and what I seek

Beyond the window, sunlight tries to break the clouds. Daylight. What do I remember? Karl came home, we talked and drank, recounted stories. I told about Michelle, and other stories. Though recollection is foggy, embarrassment burns. I can taste whisky. Smell it.

I climb out of bed, search the kitchen for confirmation of what I recall. No empty fifth of Johnnie Walker, no glasses on the counter, or in the sink. Karl's bedroom stands open, vacant, no different than ever before. As if he's never been home. But I know he was here.

In the shower, traces of water. Maybe drops left from my shower last night?

Karl's bed half-made, like usual. It's been exactly the same as this for weeks. Maybe months.

No sign of the black leather book. Maybe hidden? I could search, Karl probably won't return, catch me. But it's not something I want to find.

I feel pulled another direction. The forest wants me back. I intend to go, find Lily again. I remember every detail of her, every sensation. But which is it, something I desire, or something that desires me? A person calling to me, or a place? Am I just imposing myself where I'm not wanted?

With each step toward my next life, this old existence seems more absurdly disconnected. If I'm going to reach into the future, I can't retain my grip on the past, can't stretch far enough to span the two. Time to let go. This compelling urgency confuses me, makes me feel victim of external manipulation. How does such need arise? When the need boils up within me, I recognize it, but can't identify the source. It feels unsafe, somehow, to want so fervently. I'm unprotected, out on a limb. What I need is to convince Lily to meet me halfway, maybe make her understand what I'm asking, why I need more. Not that I want to force her into anything, but I can't help what I want.

There's a vague, lingering sense I ought to go to work today. I dismiss the idea, not even sure what day it is. Of course the odds are against me — there are more weekdays than weekends — but this morning feels like Saturday.

In the shower, I don't allow myself to think where I'm heading. Don't decide. I plan to wear something that will work either place, whether I go to work, or visit Lily. I'll get in the car and drive, and things will make sense along the way. I could check my computer or phone, see what day it is. This is my intention, something I plan to remember to do once I get dressed and I'm closer to leaving.

Somehow I forget until I'm walking up the ramp to the parking lot. My cell phone is in my pocket, but I decide not to check the calendar. I may not like what I find. As I pull out of the parking lot onto Marine Drive, I realize I'm not going to work. It's never been a true question.

The river slides past. Birds glide, sometimes dive into the water. On Government Island, clusters of people persist in camping, though the sky is overcast, the wind strong and chilly. To reach I-5, I have to pass by work. The lot is full of cars, and Constant is standing out there with a bunch of guys looking under the raised hood of his Corvette, a red 1968 Stingray. I slow, think about pulling in, but don't use my turn signal. I let off the brake, accelerate toward the highway.

I admit it. I'm addicted to pleasures that aren't even real. Lily isn't somebody I get to keep. This won't last. That's something I can accept. When I see her, I'll forget any reservations I held. Set aside fear, let need take over.

As I near the Kalama and Cayson's land, the clouds thin, penetrated by the sun's brightness.

I park outside the gate, like I've done dozens of times. No, more than that. Hundreds, thousands. This is something I've always done, every day. I've visited the river a million times. Lily can't possibly still be waiting. If she's gone, I can fish the river instead. But I find myself walking, breathing easily in the wild air, not carrying my fishing gear. I think I left it at home. This means I'm going to see Lily. She'll be here after all. The birds make sounds unlike anything I've heard before. I'm not sure. Maybe the same thought crossed my mind last time.

Walking up the driveway, I turn off earlier than usual, trying to avoid the house. The trail slips into the trees. Dew stands in luminous beads on blades of grass and fern fronds. Not far off, the river hums, a blended murmur of invisible insects.

This is the wrong trail. I want to avoid Cayson's place, but this path takes me near another building, some little fishing shack, weathered and faded, falling to ruin. The aged wood is cracked and split. Outside, like an obsoleted front yard, is a rhombus of overgrown grass. Near the center of this old lawn is a barren rectangle of packed, smooth soil, like a chalkboard on the ground covered with scratches, lines, figures. I wish I had something to write with, so I could copy down these word-like forms. I hope I'll remember to tell Lily about this. She might want to see.

I hurry past, continuing toward the river. Rather than going down the bank, I veer left, heading downriver on the parallel trail I normally use. The rest is easy, familiar. This has been my entire life. Trees change. Tall, dense Douglas Firs give way to more haphazardly arranged pines interspersed with birches, blackberry stalks, prehistoric ferns, wild rhododendrons and field grass.

I see it ahead, Lily's field. Her home. I'm still not sure what to call this. House, cabin, or what? It looks faded with age, hollow. I move closer. This place isn't just quiet. It's abandoned.

What if she's gone? If it's empty, this is all over.

"Are you lost?" A voice behind, startling.

I spin.

Lily's standing there, in a place where nobody was just seconds before. I'm not sure where she—

"You look sad," she says.

Closer still. Why am I always so maddeningly self-aware about every movement, whether toward proximity or distance? "How many times have we met?" I ask, trying to appear neither lost nor sad, as she suggests. It's strange, seeing her outside, in daylight.

"I don't know how many. I forgot to count." Lily's face changes. "But one thing I do know, it's been too long since last time. Too long."

Maybe she's right. I've been trying to keep myself away, but why? All I've desired has been to see her again. "I must have been trying to understand things better."

"There's nothing to understand," she says. "I only try to give what you want."

I believe this is true. I shouldn't focus so much on what she withholds. "I'm here now."

She leads me, though I know the way. There's never been any question I'll return, that I'll find her, and we'll go together inside. I only wonder how long I'll remain.

Inside, my eyes burn. My focus sharpens, my body surges with tingling hypersensitivity. I breathe faster. It's dark, I can barely see. Her eyes are wide, almost wild. We come together, clutching, a series of confused gestures, too-eager responses. I have no idea what either of us desires. All I know is we're here, both of us, together.

Lily moves to kiss me, blood on her lips.

Startled, I pull back. "Stop."

There's no blood.

Her mouth opens into something resembling a smile, eyes cast down as if she's played a trick. One shoulder lifts, some kind of conciliatory gesture. She flicks her straight black hair over her right shoulder, reaches for me, touches my mouth with open palms. It's awkward at first, but comes across as playful, experimental. Lily takes my right hand, extends my fingers and places my open palm lightly across her mouth, mirroring the gesture she herself just made. She hums, and the vibration tickles my skin like some exotic transmission of data, some new language. It's something I should be able to understand.

Our hands tug at clothing already damp with sweat. Breathless, we scramble sideways, fall onto the pile of blankets. Darkness deepens. Lily seizes my face in her hands, wrestles me beneath her. I remember a dream, sinking. Our bodies strain. Though I've just arrived, already my muscles burn from long exertion, my throat aches from endless raw cries. Lily guides me to that familiar place, that amniotic swim.

I no longer recall clearly the rush of my arrival, hoping for something. On the other side of that urgency, no doubt remains. No more confusion. I want to understand more of her, desire nothing more than this move into greater proximity. Lily reveals herself to me through her body, her pleasure, her books and art. With these, she holds nothing back.

Nights, days, all dark. Lacking sunlight's intrusion, it's impossible to discern passing time.

We gasp, breathe, exert. Recover in sleep.

I wake.

Lily places my hand between her legs, watches my reaction. "What word do you have for this?"

Scalding, wet and swollen. I can't stop my mind flashing to the word Michelle always used. *Cunny.* I almost say it, but stop myself. It's infantile, and anyway, it describes not part of a woman, but part of Michelle. The two are so different. No single word can fit both at once.

"This, you mean?" I grasp and probe, stalling in awareness of my need to offer a better word. "This place between your legs?"

Lily almost smiles. "You know what I mean." She waits, won't say it for me.

I'll think of a name. I'll say it for her later. But now I find myself thinking of Michelle. I hate bringing her here, into Lily's presence. That word exemplifies Michelle's stunted, dysfunctional sexuality. What does it say about me that I can't name part of Lily's body without borrowing Michelle's terminology?

"This part of you," I say, "I worship it."

Lily releases my hand, seeming satisfied. As so often happens, a discussion shift becomes something nonverbal.

All is forgotten.

Eventually I see changes in the room, various aspects. Decorations added or removed, works of art in progress. Signs of new presence, different clothing. A blanket added. Shifts in humidity, degrees of warmth. We speak of none of these things. I notice.

When I try to discern what Lily feels, where she comes from, where she's headed, she remains closed. I push, she evades. Like trying to grasp a cloud, a shape that only seems tangible. If I reach, try to grasp, the cloud vanishes as if it were never actually present.

Sometimes while Lily sleeps, I watch her, the way I know she sometimes watches me. Other times I rise, leave her undisturbed, drawing slow breaths. I explore the room, try to read pages in darkness, venture outside, observe seasons changing in the field. Here I find proof of the passage of time, growth and death and decay. Fragile ornaments hung on trees, or shapes drawn in ash and soot on barren geometries of earth. Scattered letterforms in bone, expressions in blood. Some vanish, others appear. These changes prove we are living through more than one night.

When each image is erased, I hold it in my mind forever. The next always arrives to build upon the last.

In my sleep, Lily wraps hands around my throat, blocks my breathing. I wake thinking it's a game, try to stop her, shrug her off. Her hands lock tight, unbreakable. I struggle until vision goes black. Finally I relax, fight back the spasm of resistance. No more breath. A feeling in my lungs like starvation. Need, the beginning of lust. New desire.

Breathe, awake.

The sky must be perfectly dark. The window passes no light. This pattern we've fallen into, by wordless agreement, lying close atop the blankets, touching but not too intertwined. Lily's place gets hot, as though some unseen fire burns nearby. I sleep always conscious of distant sounds, the churn of water, tonal whispers of wind between trees like a harmonious, rhythmic beating of wings. Sounds real and imagined combine to music. I still hear the Columbia rushing beneath floats and docks and other houseboats. The sounds, always the same.

Deeper now, rumbling. Not a dream. My eyes open, awake. Painfully loud, the ground vibrating.

"Lily?" I sit up, reach for her, find the space beside me empty. I search the room, can't see. A glow rises outside the grimy window. It fades, rises again. A fixed rhythm, like breathing or a heartbeat. The ebb and flow of the rumble matches the pulsing luminance. Still no movement, no hint of Lily's presence.

I rise, stagger to the door. Grip the knob, expecting heat or vibration, but find only cool metal. Bracing myself, I throw the door open. Not sure what I anticipate; some military helicopter or *Close Encounters* invasion? There's nothing to see, nothing present. The sound is quieter and more distant than I perceived. A weirdly drawn-out echo, some long-ago collision stretching into the present, louder when my memory is clearer, quieter as my recollection fades. Back and forth.

Someone asked what I would say if they told me they saw lights in the sky. Who was it, and when?

I'm up, I could go to the river, look down. Maybe the steelhead are there, holding. But what would they be waiting for, in the night?

Nothing to do but lie down, wait, maybe sleep. Out of one dream, into another. If I only wait, I'll circle back into some waking reality in which Lily exists alongside me.

Always straight from sleep into intimacy, no preamble. Our bodies breathe each other for air. Our exchanges are sometimes quiet, other times focused on specific actions with fetishistic attention to angle or detail or contortion of physiology. Most often, we build from aching need, from the fear this may never happen again, into greater urgency, heart-racing, muscle-clenching forward-moving impetus. Desire to quench, to strangle, to dominate, to expel. Then easing, languidness and brief talk. More complicated feelings arise, unspoken. Desire for elements not present here. Mixed feelings, doubt. Concepts I'm unsure how to articulate. Not only does Lily refuse to help. She wishes I'd stop. We argue over her sense of my various dissatisfactions.

I try to talk about Karl and Sadie, seeking to illustrate some point.

"Who are they?" she asks. "How does it help you or me, here, if we talk about strangers?"

"I'm looking for analogies. Trying to understand each other."

"We understand."

"Maybe you. I'm not sure I do."

"What more do I need to share?"

I'm surprised, frustrated at my inability to come up with something specific to ask her. She's offering, and I'm not sure what to tell her.

She sits up, rises to her knees as if in contemplation of standing, leaving me here. "If you don't like the way I am, the way I was when you met me, why come back? Why stay?"

"I wanted to be with you. I just can't stop myself wanting what I want." My confusion is an impasse, a dead-end. From here I can't advance, can't move forward. In such futility as this, I can only close my eyes, let go.

Relinquish.

Next time I wake, Lily is standing over me in the dark. I see her plainly, the whole room clearer than ever before, the objects and corners and surfaces clearly defined and separate from one another. I sit up, rub my eyes.

Lily holds a pen in her right hand, cradles a large brown book with her left arm. She's writing in the book, or maybe drawing. Watching me.

"What are you doing?" I ask.

"I'm not hiding anything," she says. "You can see."

"You're looking at me while you write."

"It's not about you." Her voice is flat.

I don't know what to ask. I feel sick. "Then what are you writing about?"

"I can't tell you what. I can't tell you why."

I want to know more, though I realize she doesn't want me to want this. "You have to."

She arches an eyebrow. "What you believe you want, you don't really want."

"Tell me something," I insist.

She tells me something.

"The river cuts from a dead mountain to an artery river, a direct connection." Exasperation contorts Lily's face as she speaks, as if she's resolved to reveal the most primal truths from deep in her gut. "Every river, all of them large and small, each one is connected. Water connects to water and also connects above and below. The sky, the ground. All the water everywhere."

"But that's..." I don't understand, can't make sense of it. "Is that all?" I'm trying hard not to seem disappointed.

"What, then?" Her constant refrain. She appears ready to cry, something I've never seen her do.

It's a question I can't answer. I have nothing specific. "I don't need to know everything. But something."

"What? You don't want what I offer, but some different thing. You can't tell me what I need to change to be more like what you want."

"I need to feel I'm learning about you." I realize as I speak, this is hopeless. Can't she understand this sense of lack? So many of my desires are met, but not all. I feel untethered, less than solid. Pain within me also means pain for Lily. That isn't what I want, but an unavoidable side effect.

I remember sounds Sadie made. Wild howls, unrestrained screeching, like protesting a knife twisting in her gut. I can't tell Lily this, can't convey the first hint of what it was like to hear.

I try to sleep. For the first time since I came here, I lie restless.

Something shifts outside the window, moonlight slipping beyond the grasp of clouds. Illumination spills through the window, casts silvery gray across us. Lily lies motionless, her body so fully revealed in this light, I'm startled by what I see. Her skin patterned like fabric, shiny black in places, silver in others. At first I think she must be wearing some sheer, decorated bodysuit. I follow the curve of her thigh, up her hip, across her back. The pattern continues unbroken. I search for seams, gaps, or a cuff ending at ankle, neck or wrist. She's entirely covered, fingertips, toes, eyelids. Her skin is glossy, ornately embellished, like a full-body tattoo or scarification.

What is she?

Lily stirs, as if disturbed by my scrutiny, rolls over and looks up, eyes half-lidded. Her face is more distinctly patterned than the rest. Apparently unconcerned by what I might have seen, Lily appears dreamily distracted, at best half-aware.

I stand, search for my clothes, pull on my pants.

Lily is standing, naked and pale, by the door. Her skin is smooth, white and unblemished, like always before.

"Don't misunderstand." She reaches for my face.

I stop, and let go my clothing. I don't know how I could have been so wrong, seen her so unclearly. "I'm sorry, I don't know why..."

She leads me back to the bed. I lie down, try to clear my mind.

She doesn't move for a long time, then turns, rests on her side, facing me. Her hand touches my chest. "What you want is not possible."

I want to argue that isn't true, but I know it is. "Look around here. It's all smoke." I'm not trying to change the subject. I really can't see.

"There's no smoke," Lily says. "You've been dreaming. Every time you wake up, you think whatever was happening in your dream is still going on, continuing into where you're awake. You're not very good at telling one from the other."

This judgment of hers stings a bit. I can't help being reminded of Michelle, all her criticisms of me, especially the implication that I'm the one always judging others, yet unprepared for judgment myself.

Maybe it's true.

"Tell me what you wish we could do together," Lily suggests.

I pretend to consider, but I just wish my eyes would stop stinging. I don't need to give it any thought. The answer is at the tip of my tongue, I've imagined it so many times.

"I want us to get dressed, go to my car, for a long drive along the Columbia. A sunny day, drive out the Washington side, cross Bridge of the Gods and come back on the Oregon side. Have dinner there in Hood River, if the timing's right, or maybe Salty's, right near where I live. I want people to see us together. I want you to come see where I live, Karl's place. He should see us together, and Sadie too. Maybe even for Michelle to call when we're together, and I'll pick up and tell her I can't talk, I'm with somebody else. We could sleep in my bed. It's uncomfortable, too small, but just one night. To sleep together in that room, I could undo all the nights, sleepless for so long. So much loneliness. Pain."

I stop, breathing hard. Anything else? Of course there is, but that's a start. "That would be perfect. Have you there, just sleep. Better still, I want to fuck you, hear the sounds you make. Drown out the other sounds. All the creaks and moans and sound of the river."

She's lying so still, I'm unsure whether she's considering which things might work for her, and which would not.

Then she speaks. "You want impossible things."

I try to read her voice. It sounds perfectly even, emotionless, but I don't know.

*You want impossible things.*

I want to say more, try some other angle, but decide to just wait. Rest, dream. Wake to another world.

She's doing something with my hands while I sleep. I remember our hands against each other's mouths, that strange, alien intimacy. But this isn't the same. I feel sharpness, tearing. Lily lets me sleep, strips away skin, steals fingerprints. Pulls out bones, detaches muscle, replaces these with parts she's created. Fragments of leaf, shards of bone from dead animals. Blood and guts of river fish.

I jerk awake. She's holding my hands between hers. Everything's slippery with blood. I jolt upright, scream at the sudden pain. Is this real, or remnant of a dream? Maybe she's right. I can't tell the difference between the two.

"Calm," Lily whispers.

I draw back my hands, rub them together. No blood, nothing slippery. Just skin. No pain.

What was that feeling? I'm only drifting. Sleep fixes—

Then hyperventilating, chest thumping, sweat-drenched skin. "What are you doing to me?" I ask.

"You had another dream. Shouting, tossing."

"You built my hands," I say.

"No."

"You took out my blood," I insist, aware how these words sound. "Where are my bones?"

She only stares at me, indifferent.

Didn't I promise myself I'd watch out for red flags, that if something seemed wrong, if Lily acted in a way that reminded me of what went wrong with Michelle, I'd protect myself? I have to force myself to see the way things really are.

Why won't Lily answer? I want her to say something.

I slow my breathing, try to calm myself. "I never thanked you for the book."

She appears taken by surprise, maybe even confused. At first I think she's going to say it wasn't from her, that she'll pretend not to know what I mean. Then her face relaxes, loosens into an expression of open guilelessness. Even the straight black bangs and angular eyebrows seem less severe, more girlish.

"I'm bound to offer an exchange for what you've given," Lily says.

"It's beautiful," I begin, then realize how much more it would mean if I understood the contents. "Maybe you could explain some things?"

"It's not for explaining," she says cautiously. "You already know everything you need. It will seem clearer, later."

Practical matters intrude into mind, like being nudged by a reminder. My job, my bills. All my possessions, and my room at Karl's. These things have seemed distant for so long, nearly forgotten. Now they seem pressing, urgent once more. It's alarming to consider how things might have changed since I last considered the life I left.

"You could just remain here." Lily seems capable of reading my thoughts, arguing against my unspoken doubts. "Not forever, but..."

"I can't just escape, escape, escape." After so long living a fantasy, believing myself so changed that I can leave everything behind, I realize it's not true. Yes, some things are different, but not everything. Not enough. When I try to carry Lily back to my own life, when I present her with considerations most people would accept easily, she simply can't cross that line. For her, it's impossible. I keep straining to match these two segments of my life, this magical escape and the real, practical considerations, but the gap can't be crossed. The variance refuses to balance. Just because I want it, doesn't mean it can happen. So at some point I have to return.

"I can accept never learning everything about you," I begin. "But you can't completely refuse to reveal anything at all."

"It's the same thing." Her inflection makes this sound like a question.

I want to stand, tell her I'm leaving, that I won't return. I want to say these words. Do I mean them, or am I just trying to win an argument?

"Where I'm from, you were never there," Lily says. "Where I'm going, you'll never be."

"It's so certain for you?" I try not to choke on the words. "Saying there's no future?"

"What's upsetting for you is different for me." She rests her hand on my face. This time I don't fall away into sleep. "I shift and fade like clouds. I flow like water from river to river."

"Lily, you don't have to say—"

"Some of us change, one thing to another. That's me. Others never can change."

This makes some kind of sense, though I hate to accept it. "Others like me." The reason I've fallen in so easily with Lily is the permeability of her boundaries. She's beautifully unreal, too transitory to keep, but that's the only reason we ever came together in the first place. "Like a—" I try to speak of caterpillars and pupae, but feel my face contorting in pain.

"I don't want to hurt." Her face shows no hostility. "I can only say truth."

I'm afraid I'm going to cry in front of her. This reminds me of home, of Michelle. So stupid, to be humiliated like this again. I have to go.

"I've said you can always leave, that I won't stop you." Lily's voice is gentle. "Maybe now is time."

I stand, and this time unhurriedly dress myself, facing away. She makes no effort to stop me. I fumble, putting on these clothes. I can't remember the last time I wore them.

When I turn back to Lily, I'm unsure what I'll say. "I'm not sure I'll be back." How much of this is frustration? Some of what I'm feeling must be an echo of rejection, a reminder of Michelle commanding me to leave. But this is different.

"Don't swear you'll never return." Her eyes look serious, regretful. "I already know you will."

I don't believe this, not now. All I want is to flee. So many feelings, wavering and uncertain. Whether I should leave at all, and if I do, should I leave the door open for possible return? "Lily," I begin, and say nothing more. I turn, go out the door and leave without closing it behind me.

I walk to the foot path, and only then look back. The door to Lily is shut. Her place looks dark, abandoned. Though I know she remains inside, it looks like she must already be gone, or was never really there.

I run.

When I reach the driveway, my car almost within sight, I stop. The night air chills my lungs. Tears gather in my eyes. I can't imagine why I should cry over someone I barely know. This must be more of the same, ridiculous fallout over Michelle. Even that makes no sense. I should be forgetting my wife, using my experience with Lily to put that pain into perspective.

No, I've repeated the same mistake. The two women are completely different. The problem is me. I'm susceptible. Weak.

Lily's right, I probably won't be able to stay away, but at least for now, I have to go home. I resume walking. Through the trees to my left, toward the river, light hints on the horizon. It's the first time I've seen daylight in quite a while. Seems like forever.

My car is heavy with condensed mist, lightly frosted, as if encased in a thin layer of ice. The door opens, the engine starts.

I drive, thinking not of Lily, but Michelle. Why her? Not because she remains important. I shouldn't allow myself to continue seeing her as she never was. The only reason to remember Michelle is to help myself forget Lily. In contrast to Lily's inscrutability, Michelle offers one thing Lily never could. Revelation of self, a clearly-outlined identity. Not that this ought to make Michelle appealing. She's not someone I should desire.

Where Lily is pure, blank otherness, Michelle is over-embellished, vain and fussy self-regard.

I wish the two could trade aspects, that Michelle could grant Lily that one trait, at least a less narcissistic version. Failing that, what if Michelle gained something of Lily's nature? I wish I could merge the best parts of each, though I realize this is unfair, unrealistic. I have my own failings. It's unreasonable to expect perfection in others.

It's fine to understand this, but where does that leave me? Alone, driving home in the dark, feeling less certain than ever before what I ought to try to be.

# Chapter 19

### The clarity and confusion of waking dreams

Home doesn't feel like home. I repeat the word to myself, trying to extract from it some semblance of comfort.

Of course Karl's gone. When I want solitude, he's home. When I want company, he's away weeks at a time.

The sound of this river is driving me insane. What am I supposed to do? I'm determined not to backslide, won't allow myself to return to the state I was in before Lily. Rather than be alone, I should go somewhere public. A bar, or a restaurant. Salty's sounds good, just down the river, but I was just mentioning the place to Lily. If I go there, it will be impossible to think of anything but her.

How long since I've eaten? My guts ache.

No, I won't leave, not until I get some sleep. When I was with Lily I thought I was getting sleep, but it was never restful, always interrupted. My brain feels intoxicated, half-poisoned.

I undress, climb into bed, feeling anxious. I try to close my eyes.

Soon I realize this isn't going to happen. I can't stop myself thinking about getting up, looking out windows, down the hall, toward Karl's room. I lie in bed, picturing myself standing in the hall outside Karl's room, staring into the dark, straining to see. What am I looking for? This obsession is getting me nowhere. It makes no sense. If I could only get some rest, I might wake up feeling better, then maybe tomorrow start trying to get over this.

If only. But my broken mind, all my ruinous impulses prevent it. I grind my teeth until my jaw aches. So much anger. Where does it all come from?

First, I need to stop thinking of Lily.

And no more Michelle. She's dead to me.

Also, forget Sadie. I barely even know her. There's no reason a stranger should be echoing around in my mind.

From a perspective outside myself, I see someone who resembles me sitting up, rising from this bed, moving through a dark room in a trance. Called by sirens, seduced by nameless, faceless possibilities.

*Who are they? What are their names?*

Dream myself backward, spiral through time, drift toward yet another loss. Bodiless mind, looking down from high above, scrutinizing the corpus once occupied. Eyes outside my former blunt corpus motionless in a field of grass. Dream a downward rush, swoop out of the sky, strike the body with such force it jolts as if startled. Occupy it again, neither dead nor sleeping, but restless beneath a clear sky. Other stars watch, wait.

*Go to her, you can go back. Give yourself over.*

I wake in time to struggle against hands pressing down my face and chest, forcing me deeper into malleable ground. Fight back, struggle to pull apart the fingers. See the face, the woman on top of me. A crescent smile, gleaming bright and madly charming. Grinning Sadie presses down, crushes me into the earth. Half-submerged, I feel her skin slide against mine. Slippery as if oiled, her touch conveying a dream's exaggerated pleasure. Urgent need, convulsive stimulus. Despite all she's doing to remove me from this world, I want to possess her. No thought for Lily or Michelle or Karl. Just my own desire to feel that slick, tingling, nettle-stung flesh.

I recede willingly into the ground. I accept my subsidence. Relax. Give in.

The woman stands back, moves away, her smile knowing. I see her face, a stranger. Not Sadie after all.

The wide earth narrows, closes over me.

*I'm buried.*

I awaken, eyes sharp, light piercing. I've been dreaming. So often I think I can't sleep, that I'm tortured by insomnia, yet hours pass and somehow I experience new dreams. I lie awake, plan and shift, dreaming with eyes open. My stomach burns. I wake feeling death near, afraid insanity might take me. This is how I shift the world so I might survive.

Sleep in stealth, invent solutions. Wake, find desires met.

If I have to actually close my eyes and let go, I'll just dream myself backward. Out of this, back to where I was before. Count my losses, then what? Identity shifts according to need. Mine, hers.

None of this will change her mind.

I found my antidote, created her. Lily came to fill my need, invented for that purpose. She doesn't say the words I want to hear, but her voice calms, her body soothes in the moment. Lily's contour, her texture, skin buttery slick, always damp. Sweat glistens, a mist of fragrant oil. Her form only a costume, no person inside.

Eyes close. Mouth opens. What's within? Hollowness. A tangle of endless string, a lock never keyed.

I've always thought there was some value in possessing truth. That's wrong. There's no point unless I can control myself. She takes from me while I'm not looking, eyes shut, dreaming of coming days. She pulls me into her while I'm adrift, opens me, removes bones, drains blood, distills from these words a tale yet untold.

Lies motionless beneath, her fingers flicking, prodding, choosing.

My eyes are closed. She steals eyes from beneath twitching lids.

My lips don't speak. She tears loose my lips, stows them away.

My hands have nothing to do. She breaks fingers, splits each into a word.

She breathes into my twitching fingerless palm, imprints her secrets. I know what she does to me, though I always forget.

Ugh, these sheets stick to me. I'm drenched in sweat. Sit up, coughing. This room is smoky, claustrophobic. Stand up, look around confused. Where am I? Is this another deeper level of dream?

No, this is really happening. My room in Karl's houseboat.

It's not sounds that awaken me, like before, but a smell of burning. I panic out of sleep, bit by smoke. Bolt out of bed, and stand shivering, heart pounding. No fire here, only a smell like smothered campfire.

Smell of smoke is manifestation of the persistent terror that flames may arise from nothing.

Out to the hall, searching. The empty house, bright with morning. Scan the living room, the kitchen. Beyond both windows, flat gray sky gives hard rain. Back to Karl's bedroom, open and vacant. His bed, uncharacteristically made. Here, that smell of burning is strongest.

Go in, look closer.

This is real. I'm actually awake, standing here. Karl's room, just like that other night, but it's daylight.

The bed isn't made. It's stripped, a bare mattress. The headboard shelf, where Karl always stored a half-dozen motivational books with titles containing words like "success," and "winner," and "dreams," no longer contains any books. Nothing on the shelf but a mound of white ash. That must be the source of that smell. There's no sign of heat, no burn marks. I poke a finger into the ash, find it insubstantial, the way cigarette ash appears solid but breaks at the touch.

It's not only the stripped bed that's unusual. Karl's whole room is vacant. Clothes gone, luggage. Though his dresser remains against the wall, all the drawers are open, empty. In the bathroom, Karl's kit is absent, toothpaste and toothbrush, shampoo, razor and towel, all missing. Only the bar of soap in the shower remains.

I return to my room. There the smell persists, like neutral incense. I check under the mattress, where I stashed my book. Nothing remains of it but the same white ash, flattened to nothing. No book, as if it burned away without fire. This leaves me confused, afraid. What can I do against this? I want to understand. Does everyone but me know what's happening? When Karl saw my book, he didn't recognize it, despite possessing one nearly identical. Now I wish I'd asked directly, not only hinted around, hoping for some reaction.

Sadie was curious about the book, kept emphasizing the value of such a gift. She said it proved my value to the giver.

I can't expect Sadie to provide answers.

But the giver of the gift. Lily.

If Lily came to me here, could I resist? I wish I had power over my impulses, but I don't. Though I might blame this on lust, the problem is wider. Michelle's hold on me had nothing to do with sex. Toward the end of our marriage, I forgot what little I ever knew of navigating desire. Emasculation weakened my resolve until I was incapable of action. Michelle's suffering must have exceeded my own. At least she managed to break loose our frozen stalemate.

Maybe Lily did the same. I can't see the situation clearly enough to be sure.

I want Karl to tell me about his book. I wonder if he knows where it came from. If he were here, I'd be direct, refuse to accept evasion or non-answers. But the way things look, I'm not sure Karl will return.

I can't wait around. I shower, dress quickly.

Outside, I run along the docks, up ramps. Through dense, chilling rain, to my car.

I can't ask Karl. Only Lily knows. This time, it will be different.

I'll face her calmly, won't fall into her bed, won't even let her close the door. That's what I should've done before, insisted she answer my questions. No matter what she tries, I won't allow any distractions, won't be turned sideways, spun around, or confused.

This time will be different.

# Chapter 20

### I return to the field

I race back, driving blind, to the place I never should have left.

Now I realize, although I'm breaking my resolve to stay away, it's not my fault. I'm being influenced from outside. A storm grows, clouds thickening on the horizon. My car struggles against surging wind. All the world blurs, everything outside pulled out of shape, smeared by rain falling thick as oil. An invisible hand pushes me back, trying to prevent my return.

Every aspect like a dream in which the very universe frustrates and impedes.

I park beside River Road, outside Cayson's gate. Some part of me believes I may never return. I slip through the barrier and begin to run up the driveway. Trees moan and sway in the violent wind. Limbs crack and fall amid a sprinkle of blown needles. Though I come here seeking, already I understand I won't likely receive the concrete and straightforward answers I desire. The best I can hope is to receive vague and poetic hints of the same kind that left me dissatisfied before.

So why do this? Why come here? Because it's all that's left.

Even beneath a canopy of trees disintegrating in the storm, rain bites my face, stings my eyes. Summer is over. I should have remembered my jacket, but it's been months since I've worn one.

Up the driveway, instead of splitting off where the first trail forks toward the river's more active upper section, I continue nearer Cayson's house, paralleling the riverside path. I want to run directly to Lily, would rather leave the shelter of forest, even amid this raging weather, than approach those older trees near the house, cut with lines dripping red. That area surrounding the big house still makes me nervous.

Fatigue overcomes me and I slow to a walk, breathing hard, squinting against hammering rain. So tired. I have to overcome, try to run again. Walking won't bring me there fast enough. The cabin is still a quarter mile away.

A deep boom resounds somewhere ahead, close enough to feel, though I see no source or cause. The ground rumbles as if from an explosion or lightning strike. My ears pop at the atmospheric shift. Terrified, I resume running, despite knowing I should run away from this, rather than toward it. Fear exhilarates, drives me onward with new urgency. I want to meet whatever my future may be. Leaves swirl, trees bob and heave, cracking. I fight against the surge of wet torrents more solid than wind. The world feels like it's falling apart.

Everything appears changed. The gap between forest to my left and river to my right broadens. Ahead the land flattens. Not far now to the final ridge of thin trees, swaying wildly, some damaged. The final corner before Lily's field. Wild blackberry stalks form a barrier, tangled and probing into the ground through a tumble of old cracked and weathered stones from a long-ago time when the river was much higher.

This is it, the final verge. This is where Lily waits.

I stop, gasping with exertion and maybe fear. Rain trickles down my face, streams into my mouth and down my chin. I step forward once, cross the threshold of the invisible line extending from the sharp point where trees and brush come to an end.

I step into the open, fully revealed, seeking too much to articulate.

Instead, I find nothing. The cabin is gone. No trace of Lily's presence, no discernible sign she's ever been here. The field is transformed, all shapes and proportions are wrong. Grass once lush green is now sparse, bleakly yellowish, the ground muddy. Perimeter trees have shifted back, relocated. The field no longer sags in the middle, as if beneath the weight of Lily's A-frame. That low center point is not only vacant, but somehow rests higher, raised to the level of the ground where I stand.

I look around confused, trying to believe I've found the wrong field. Maybe there are different places that look similar. This must be a mistake.

"Lily?" My voice thin, feeble.

I scan the field and surrounding forest, knowing I can't be wrong, but hoping. What have I missed?

In the center, in the place where Lily's house always stood, all that remains is a rectangular footprint of bare, wet soil surrounded by grass. This is the spot where Lily was always waiting for me. I wish I could have understood her better, been more receptive to what she was trying to give. If I could have read the book, grasped its messages, I might have been able to accept what she offered. Now it's too late. Too late to understand, and too late to find her.

I kneel. This bare rectangle, imprint of what I came expecting to find. The only hint of what's missing, virginal ground protected from seasons of long years beneath the foundation of a home, somehow vanished. This spot might be twenty feet by ten. What do I expect scrutiny to reveal? Some fossil record or organic trace? A final message left behind?

Michelle should've been lesson enough. What I pursue is never what I hope for. Why should I be shocked, finding Lily gone? From the beginning, from that first day I walked by, I've guessed wrong about everything. Every certainty, always mistaken. Lily herself. Her room, her books and art. All lost.

I study the ground, looking for footprints, indentations, anything to indicate where I slept beside her. It seems like months, years ago. What is this place, equidistant between trees behind and river ahead?

The raindrops dance in puddles, seep into the earth, return to the river. I touch the bare ground and look straight up. Clouds above, impenetrable gray. I have no sense what's beyond, what shape the sky makes above this weather. The clouds give rain to pierce my eyes, to wash away stains. In this ground I find no remnant of any past structure, nothing dissolved or burned or rotted with age. No fragments, no ash. Maybe a smell of burning, mostly washed clean by tireless rain. As I crawl nearer the edge of the rectangle, just before the grass perimeter I see black upright shapes, hints of living matter. Slippery mushrooms, dead phallic tongues reaching toward an indifferent sky. As I reach to pluck one of the mushrooms, I see other organic materials, detritus mixed with soil, an infinity of detail I can only discern once I move closer. My eyes reach, and adjust. Shards of dark substance, previously invisible heaps of crushed bone, tangles of shredded hair. The soil here is mostly blood. The closer I look, the deeper I go, the more details I discover.

My vision wasn't prepared, before. Now I see.

A hollow shape, crumbling burnt umber wax, some lesser shape escaped from within. At the center of the vacancy stand dark needles like upright fish bones intermingled with bits of blood-slick leaf. The rib cage or shell of some vague thing once alive, impossible to identify, so long dead it's transformed into something else, like petrified wood. A human-shaped carapace, implication of skin hollowed and broken. A shell someone might wear and discard once cracked, hard outside yet inside sticky with microscopic life. Tiny shapes, flesh-soft, pulpy fragments within an amniotic membrane.

Look closer.

An infantile form tears free, a shroud imprinted with phantom words still echoing. All the language that ever came to mind, gone, carried away. A womb wrecked and abandoned. A shell, once a woman. Is this all she was, the body she wore and left behind? When I touched Lily, this is what she was made of. When I kissed, tasted, penetrated, slept beside her, was Lily only a shell, a blank screen on which I projected my own image? Not tangible, only apparently solid, and only pleasurable to touch because I made her that way? Never fully real?

Blood and sticks, dirt and leaves. A skeleton built of bones long dead.

If I can't read the book, or understand the woman who gave it, how can I hope to know why she chose me?

I don't understand myself well enough to guess.

She gave the book, took it away. Gave herself to me, drew me back one last time. Now this.

I need to get away. Never come back. After this, no more. Nothing remains for me here but decaying bits, a mixture of things dead and nameless. I stand, try to wipe my hands clean of black mud, at once gritty and slick. Take a single step, then stop. Which way? There's still the river, the canyon. With all this rain, the pool won't be transparent, the way I remember.

I feel no desire to return home, no identifiable impetus of any kind. I only know I can't stay here.

Instead, I turn to face the wall of trees. No trails are visible, but there's room to explore, among the trees between Cayson's place and the road. Maybe I'll find the way Lily came and went. Some pathway or clearing, even a place to park a car. Then before I leave, I'll stop by Cayson's house, one final time. I'll keep a discreet distance. For some reason, I feel like someone might finally be home.

Into the forest.

High-stepping to avoid the tangle of ferns and vines underfoot, I lurch deeper, toward where I imagine River Road must be. There's no way to measure distance or direction here, with no milestones but a million identical trees. I walk a long time, trying to follow a straight line, but find no road. Nothing but featureless forest in undifferentiated repetition, as if the same trees and moss and ferns have reproduced to take over the world. Rain no longer falls, or if it does, I can't feel it here, but wind still presses against me, insistent. Wind shoves aside one season for the next, one phase of life for another. Wind moves over the world's surface, making sounds through trees so suggestive of space and dimension, I believe I could close my eyes and identify the relative locations and sizes of every trunk and branch all around me. I close my eyes, keep walking. Try to trace where Lily might have gone, imagine the line she took. Envision her passage, feel what drove her. Did she hide a car on some driveway or fire lane hidden among the trees?

A shape intrudes, heard rather than seen. The wind moves not only through trees, but another form. I can feel the presence, somebody walking through the forest alongside me. Someone else, searching.

I open my eyes, see movement to my left, in the corner of my vision. Wood cracks underfoot, then running steps sound. I spin, ready to flee or chase, but my eyes find no confirmation of what I heard. Sounds of movement, but nothing to see. Wind rises, a smell of burning leaves. I veer left, thinking to cut directly back to my car, and hurry through trees. Time to get the hell out of here. Run.

Instead of finding the road or my car, I encounter something else. Another house. I emerge from the trees, see the whole place revealed. Not Cayson's white-painted modern wood construction, but something much older. The gray stone facade is wet, blotchy with black fungus and white lichen. A circle of uneven paving stones surrounds what must have been a double entry door, surmounted by stone ornamentation, strange pagan or gothic shape patterns, and an open-mouthed stone face textured like tree bark and stained green with moss. The doors have been blocked shut by a rough masonry of coarse lime plaster holding together brown and grey river rock. On the ground to the left of the paving stones is a circular arrangement, an ornamental labyrinth of black gravel built up with small white standing stones.

I find this place terrifying, so unlike Cayson's conventional home nearby. Old as a castle, suggestive of a far distant place and an earlier time. At once fascinated and afraid, I approach, veering left to avoid the labyrinth. It might be forty feet in diameter, with barrier walls low enough to step over and walk straight across, but its careful arrangement seems meaningful, as if it bears some kind of ceremonial significance. It's something I'd rather avoid.

At the left front corner of the house, finally able to see around the side, I'm surprised to see the stone facade giving way to modern wood siding, painted white, and a wooden deck on the second story. I realize what I'm seeing, the connection between two very different places. This isn't a second house in Cayson's forest. It's the other side of the same house. I've only ever approached from the driveway or on the way back from Lily's field. This isn't a home with a front and a rear, but within a single structure, two entirely different aspects. A newer façade greets those coming up the driveway or from the river, while an older face looks out into the trees.

I take shelter beneath the upper deck, hiding from rain and cold wind, trying to decide what comes next.

From the small ground-level deck on which I stood before when I looked in through the kitchen window, stairs angle up. The top deck wraps around the newer half of the house. Instinctively I keep toward this side, which is more familiar, like my own house. It seems like a place I could live. I'm less comfortable with the strange, old world aspect. Even seeing it, I have a hard time imagining this as a single, connected structure.

I climb the stairs, thinking to check the upper windows, get a sense of what's inside. Once long ago, I peeked into the kitchen downstairs, and dismissed what I saw without bothering to look closely. I had no idea this facade concealed any secrets. I wonder what might be hidden inside.

The deck doesn't reach as far as the stone side, which has no true windows, just a few slits filled-in with ornamental colored glass, cracked and distorted. The white painted side has many windows upstairs. I try to open every one, but find them all locked. If I found a way, I'd climb inside. I want to get in, but don't want to break the glass. Rain and weather blowing through the house could destroy it.

I descend to the lower deck and again check the patio door. I tug the handle, pull hard, hoping the latch might give. At the moment I consciously wonder whether I'm willing to break the glass, the latch cracks and the door slides open.

Inside, the place is warm and dry. Shelter. The floors are pale hardwood, the walls dark green. There's no furniture, just open floors and featureless walls. The only illumination is what enters through windows. At the room's far end, a hallway opens off to the left. I'm tempted to explore, but instead sit on the floor, leaning against the wall.

It's wonderful, sitting still for a change. Something about the emptiness and quiet of this place reminds me of my house, the one I bought with Michelle. Those days before we moved in, everything a blank slate. Pure potential. I can't remember the last time my mind was so peaceful. I'll rest a while, warm up, clear my head, then make some kind of plan. It won't hurt anything to close my eyes, just for a second.

I jump alert, eyes wide. Was I falling asleep? The idea frightens me. I'm vulnerable, intruding here. Someone might come along, catch me.

But I want to stay. Nobody has visited here, not in a long time. I could hide forever. Nobody will ever come.

I rise, knees creaking, back stiff. It's almost dark. I must've slept. This room is so familiar, exactly like my old living room. That's Michelle's now, decorated with things I helped pay for. There must be other rooms, things to see. Maybe it's not all empty. Time to explore. If I'm ever going to look around, I'd better do it while I can see a little.

I edge toward the corner hallway. Coming out of the dark, I see a glow. In the hall, a dim illumination sprays from the first doorway to the right. A spill of dim orange, like a dying fire. On a wall shelf, some convoluted shape, like a tangled root turning in upon itself. The walls are changing color, gold and brown, textured like a pattern of webbing or honeycomb reaching up to the ceiling where textures meet in a seam.

This inner door is half open, marked by an ornament of silver metal and white opal. A central white sphere, a full moon between two crescents facing away from center. Within the room a candle flickers. My shadow leaps and jitters on the wall beside me. Just inside, on a glass table with a single chair of raw dark wood, stands a sphere of glossy black shot through with seams of white, like a crystal ball of opaque mineral. The far wall is decorated with three red painted symbols, which remind me of Lily's art. The outer two are the icons on the cover of my book, and Karl's. The third, central image is something I know I've seen. I don't remember where.

What is this place? It's so unlike the entry room, or the kitchen I saw previously. This realization, that I've entered a part of the structure unlike any place I've seen before, outside the boundaries of my understanding, this is the beginning of fear.

I shouldn't be here. Not my place. I feel an urge to run and at the same time fear I'll be unable to leave.

A sound behind, footsteps. I spin, realize the sound comes not from nearby, not inside, but outside the house.

Rustling of damp leaves.

I return to the entry room, go to the sliding door and stand where I can't be seen through the glass. Everything is dark, but I want to be cautious. Outside, the world is night, an idea that terrifies me. Now that it's dark, I remember what's just outside this door. That particular tree, hollow inside, its bark cut and decorated red. Hung with ornaments, bone and sinew.

I try to see what's out there, but find nothing. Silently as I can manage, I slide the door open an inch.

"Lily?" I whisper, hoping to be heard and not to be heard.

Nothing.

I open the door fully, greeted by cold wind. At least the rain has stopped. I step onto the deck. "Is anybody there?"

Still no response. I wait, listen, but I'm alone. The wind sounds hollow.

I turn, start back inside. As I reach the door, I hear the rustling again, behind me, near the hollow tree. Just like before, someone on the opposite side, always out of view, forever hiding.

Now it's too dark to see. I consider escape, but it's also too dark to run without falling, whether I head into the trees, or straight down the driveway. I'm tired of being afraid, always running, evading. Instead, I prepare myself for trouble. The possibility of violence.

I turn to face the hollow tree, step closer. Though I see almost nothing, I keep my eyes open wide, ready for whatever may come. The commotion, shuffling from the opposite side, diminishes, goes silent. I stand still, waiting. Still nothing. If I wanted to, I could convince myself I only ever imagined the sound. Nobody's here.

"Mr. Cayson?" I whisper. "I came with someone who knows you. Karl brought me here." It's a feeble excuse, but better than nothing.

No response. Of course this isn't Cayson. Must be someone else. Who?

It might be Lily.

This possibility compels a wrenching eagerness within me. "Is it you?" I blurt, voice high and desperate.

Leaves shuffle. The wind breathes.

"Why couldn't you stay sleeping?" The voice is a man's, older and rough-edged. His tone uneven, tremulous, as if he's drunk or unhinged.

I can't imagine any good reply. "You're not Cayson?"

I'm not sure, but I think I see a shape step from behind the tree, half-revealed.

"Cayson?" He takes rapid breaths in succession, like brief hyperventilation, then murmurs several nonsensical syllables before speaking clearly again. "That man's gone, a long ways, a long time. But I do think I know you."

"No, you don't." I should leave it at that. I should go. "It's dark here. We can't see each other."

"That's just it." The man seems settled, convinced. "I recognize you, good and sharp. Memory's clear as daylight."

"No." I feel a sense of threat, expect any moment to be struck out of blind darkness. "No. That's crazy. Delusional."

"Confused, maybe. We all are." Something in his voice sounds familiar. He stretches out words, enunciates slowly, almost a drawl. "But not delusional."

"Who are you?" I ask. Not Cayson, but somebody, some name I should know. Then it hits me, it's Karl, out of his mind, detached from home and job. I can't imagine why he would come here. "Is it — Is that you?" I don't dare speak the name. Of course this isn't him, isn't Karl. This man's too old. I have a problem keeping identities straight.

"I'm going," I tell the man. "You can keep this place."

"No. You stay."

This voice could belong to anybody, in such pure dark.

"Listen to what I say. I need to tell." His slow enunciations pick up speed, become a rant, as his words go unclear.

I don't understand. "Stop it," I tell him.

Then I start to understand. The man spews a litany of betrayals. Acts of violence, transgressions against love and friendship. So many sins, so much pain inflicted. I remember that night, when Karl asked the worst thing I've done. Then Karl told me about his cousin. That was my story, just like this.

"I don't want to hear," I insist, backing away. "I'm just going to leave."

"No, you stay," he says again, not listening. "And one opened herself, and I bent her round my fist."

"Stop!" I step backward, trip over the edge of the lower deck, sprawl on my back and hit my head.

"And one wanted a knife up in her, and I gave her what she needed."

I sit up, shaking my head, trying to see past all the stars.

When finally I stagger to my feet, I see his shape before me, hunched in the dark. I move right, he jumps into my path. I hesitate, then decide. I lunge, shove both hands into the man's chest. He flails back, falls, lets out a moan, more disappointment than injury. He stands, comes again. I swing, my elbow makes contact with his jaw.

Teeth clack together. He thumps to the ground again, moaning. This time he doesn't get up. I can't see his face, but kneel over his chest.

"I told you stop." I strike where I think his face must be. Keep hitting, alternating fists.

"You still are," he says, spitting blood. "Still looking."

I stop. "What did you say?"

Moonlight spills from behind clouds, revealing. I see an old man, a stranger's face bruised purple, nose and mouth running blood. Blood in his hair, streaming into his eyes, the side of his neck. Exhalation comes with a wheeze, and fresh blood sputters from his lips. He reaches with a trembling, misshapen hand, trying to wipe his face, manages only to smear the blood. His lips a black-red streak, face a dying mask. He looks at some point above himself, up in the branches of the tree. His mouth quivers. "You'll remember."

I follow his gaze, see the marked tree above us. Somehow we've turned around, ended up beneath it. All these lines have meaning, made long ago. Lily tried to tell me these shapes.

"It's hard doing both at once," the old man says. "Finding and hiding."

I crawl away, kneel beyond arm's reach.

"I'm not." I stand, turn. I'm going to leave this house, the old hollow tree, all the signs and the river. I need to get home.

"Wait, my bones broke," he rasps, struggling to breathe. "You stay."

I run toward what I think is the driveway. I come upon three more gnarled trees, not the same one I just left behind, but similar. This trio seems arranged. I don't pause to look, but can't avoid seeing the cuts in the bark. Slashes in red, adorned with white dots.

Some things are clear even in darkness.

I swerve, cross the yard to the driveway, and run without looking back. An accident of moonlight reveals a shape in the trees, a great stone statue, Pan or some other horned god of dark violence, arms aloft, head tossed sideways in revelry or mockery, his front thick with green moss slick with today's rain. I feel his notice as I run past.

For the first time, I find the gate open. My car, half blocking the way, is blanketed green with pine branches, needles, and leaves, all the fallen detritus of the storm finally passing.

# Chapter 21

### All is past

I drive back to the only place I can call home, Karl's houseboat on the Columbia.

Still no sign of Karl. The home stands vacant, other than my few possessions. Looking at it this way, it's possible to imagine nobody has ever lived here but me. I'm meant to be this way. Everybody in my life disappears, vanished into time. Every moment flits out of tangibility with the passing of the instant. I'm not sure what exactly we call existence, if nothing solid lingers.

This can't be Karl's place without Karl's presence. I remain, so this becomes mine. If I leave, what then?

I haven't forgotten rules, laws, contracts, obligations. These things exist because everyone believes in them. I keep waiting for somebody to come along, let me know it's time to go. Each time I hear someone creaking along the dock, I wonder if it's the marina manager coming to put all this to an end. Maybe she'll ask for some fee or assessment. At least ask after Karl.

If someone does come looking, what answer can I give? My only guess is that whatever enigma Karl chased led him away, toward his own fields, his own river. Both Karl and I keep secret our own mysteries, but mine led me back here. Otherwise, despite Sadie and Lily wearing bodies of contrasting shape and color, and speaking in different voices, the two are the same.

Time passes. Nobody ever comes to ask about Karl, or anything else. Every charge must have been paid ahead, well in advance. After what seems like weeks, I start leaving the front door open, despite wind and damp, hoping some passerby will be curious enough to look inside. I'm ready for someone to appear, but people rarely come this far. My house is docked at the end of the row, the marina's outermost edge, nearest the Washington side. The few who come out this far never look inside. They continue to the dead end, maybe stop a moment, then turn around and go back. It's as if nobody ever sees me.

My eyes remain open. This world may be considered a tangible realm, but the only experiences worth keeping happen elsewhere, in another line of existence. People are never the way I imagine them to be. All the give and take of pain, it's nothing but phantom sensation. I'm left with nothing but memories of pleasure, memories of suffering, not the things themselves. Exchanges on a physical level leave no trace. Even words are transient. Intimacy seems profound in the moment, as if it might endure forever, but blink and it evaporates.

In the mirror, everything is invisible. The mirror always looks behind.

Karl vanishes, so I barely remember him. I'm left with no more of Karl than of Michelle or Lily, or my books and music, my job, anything else.

The only thing kept is memory. Transience isn't something to be wished against or overcome. It's the only possibility, an absolute limit. To live through experience, what does that mean? Life passes so quickly, it's impossible to react in time. The now can never be preserved, always vanishes before a snapshot can be stolen. Is this life, that fleeting now, or is real living actually the process of sorting through the pieces later? I focus on assembling and shaping all I've been through. Finally I have time. Sensations left behind, words spoken, a book loaded with all the designs of life. It might be the most meaningful thing I ever possessed, yet while I held it, I was never able to focus without distraction. Always looking away, thinking elsewhere.

Lily made it for me. I possessed the book even if I never possessed the woman herself. She's gone. Now that I have time, I want to make sense of this. If I can sort the ideas, every page still exists in mind. Every image is a painting in memory.

I assemble paper, pens, begin scribbling notes, sketches. I'm disappointed to find the designs are only vivid so long as they remain held in imagination. Reproduced on paper, ideas fall flat. The problem isn't my lack of skill with a pen. It's more the general problem of translation. Concepts held in mind remain fluid, malleable and complex. When an idea is forcibly conformed to hard-edged concreteness, the change in language discards most of what I remember.

My plan is no longer to render on paper. Instead, I plan to create a full concept of the book, to be held in mind. It should be possible to see every page, to refine my sense of all that appears within, before moving to the next. But I'm afraid before I reach the end I may lose some details from the beginning, forget that I've forgotten. It may not be possible for imagination and memory to correlate all aspects of everything I've seen.

Soon I may need to leave the houseboat. Increasingly things are moved or rearranged in frustrating ways. Changes occur, not effected by me. Sometimes I wonder if Karl has come home, disrupted things. I'm aware of the fact that he's gone, but sometimes I wonder if this truth is as indefinite as the rest. Once in a while, this becomes a different place. A home has moods and emotions, like a person. Time changes me, and so my surroundings are also changed.

In the bathroom, I find everything disturbed. The light switch by the door is gone, and instead of a single overhead bulb, many tiny pinpoints of light aim straight at me, through the mirror from behind. These operate by knobs and switches in a flexible cluster behind the sink. When I reach for the switches, water spurts or sprays, threatening to engage my hands in some disaster of running water and electrical high-voltage. Even when I determine the system, the correspondence between switch and light, I find most of them don't turn on after all, or they flicker off again without my interference.

Finding the bathroom changed like this, without warning, I vibrate with anger. I want to complain to someone, maybe the marina manager. But Karl owns this house. The marina's just responsible for docks, utilities and parking. Nobody can fix this but me. Karl's no longer any help. I'm angry enough now that if Karl returned, I'd tell him it's crazy what he's allowed to happen. Lights impossible to control, electric switches sprayed with water. But he's not here, and anyway I have this horrible feeling that if he did show up, suddenly everything, the bathroom, the problems with the lights, the noises I keep hearing from his room, all these details would immediately revert to the way they were before. It's predictable.

I discover a note Karl left behind, which purports to explain his absence. The letter seems fake, like something I might compose myself. Nothing about it is convincing. Phony apologies, stilted formality, no resemblance to Karl's real style. Even my memory of that I've begun to question.

After the food is gone, I take this letter out to the end of the dock and let it drift away. Floating on the surface it slowly absorbs the river's substance. The paper vanishes downstream before it sinks.

I'm learning to understand what's actually real and what only seems. I try not to consider what this fakery reveals of me, especially when my subconscious manifests material changes into the world, out of my own compulsions or perverse hypothetical visions. It's hard for a person not to wish, to pretend nothing's wrong when circumstances might be shifted to make existence more bearable. Desire is painful. Urges for companionship, sex and food are profound. Is any of this my fault? Somehow I feel ridiculous, all this illusion rising out of me, like a lie told to myself, but I can't stop it. I have no power over my desires, have never possessed the capacity to restrain myself. Why should I? Nothing like that matters. Even the greatest intimacy leaves no evidence of the connection that was. Whatever passes between two people is immaterial. Everything given and received vanishes.

All that Lily bestowed is gone, but if I close my eyes, I possess everything. I hold the book in mind, turn pages, linger over uncountable images, boundless ideas. Piece together crucial connections, previously missed.

Secret names for rivers.

The history of Cayson's house.

Locations of hidden pathways.

Art forms and languages for wilderness.

Gathering places downriver.

Charts of blood runes and sigils.

I build upon these beginnings, work toward increasing understanding, the way a crossword puzzle becomes easier with every new word filled in. Hints build upon hints, toward full comprehension. Language is a code.

Now it becomes possible to imagine myself going to this place, learning the way, discovering locales invisible and unattainable to others. Unexplored fields on the shores of foreign rivers obscured from the world's view. One day I will discover Lily, though she must be a transformed person now. Dressed differently, hair changed, a different angle to her smile. Some new texture of skin. Gathering strange specimens, bits of leaf or sunbleached bone, components for new books.

With her, a small child, the only thing she ever needed of me. A little boy, not a baby, but surprisingly older. I believe this is what she took, though the math doesn't work for the child to be mine. Not enough time has elapsed for one conceived between Lily and me, in our small window of time together, to be born and to grow to this size. But now I know enough to trust that impossibility is not proof that something does not exist.

Though I haven't seen any of it yet, all this must be true.

Different as Karl and I have always been, and though I dismissed his presumptuous advice, I find myself wishing he might return. I envision him strutting through the front door, smirking, loose in the shoulders, full of innuendo and quick to offer blithe, careless opinions. His suggestions weren't compelling for their insight, yet his easy confidence was spellbinding. Even now, Karl might give me direction I could use. Whether I do as he suggests or the opposite, I would be relieved to find him returned.

After spending so much time alone, I consider the possibility of visiting Constant. Of course he wouldn't rehire me to do the work I did before. I wonder if he might offer me some other job, hard labor or graveyard work. This is foolish, a recurrence of my old weakness. I have this tendency to drift back toward the familiar. The truth is, if I made a list of any job I might possibly do, working CAD and 3D for Constant Marine would rank near the bottom. I could do so many other things, now that everyone has left me behind. First Michelle, then Lily, Karl and Sadie.

One other person has drifted away. The old Guy. For so long I wanted to be rid of him. I remember how bad things were, when I was him. I won't forget.

Memory is important, but it's not everything. Nothing replaces the flesh for immediate sensations. Real-time experiences, face to face, that's the nearest approach to ecstasy. That passion requires body, but I don't believe the physical aspect matters as much. Physicality doesn't last. All senses mislead.

Colors, words, shapes and smells. All transform, enlighten, feed the mind. I wish I still possessed my book. Now all that remains is memory of the thing, and whatever else memory has allowed me to create. I go beyond remembering what I saw, felt and smelled. I imagine further. The fewer material objects I possess, the more memory suffices. I catch myself dreaming of escape, disappearing into trees. In mind, I travel back, grasping for the past. Each time I revisit the book, I improve it. Journey through, pages growing more distinct, images clearer, ideas sharper.

When I study the section on charms, reflect on what it tells, I begin to understand how Lily reached out, changed me from a distance, even as I was unable to change myself. She lent me strength. I gained more than I lost.

I question my idealization of Michelle, and my sexual dreams of Sadie. Maybe these were a kind of test, delusions arisen on the cusp of my meeting Lily at my lowest, most vulnerable point. The women I actually knew, and in some sense possessed, what of them? Interludes with Lily, decades with Michelle. If anything remains, it's not tangible. Nothing I can see or hold.

The thing is this: More and more, even memory is my own creation.

So I continue to study, to recollect details from a book I no longer possess. I visualize colorful drawings, intuit understanding of blocks of text previously incomprehensible. Gradually I come to understand more clearly than when I held the book in my hands. I realize what Lily intended. She meant to create life, to decide within her pages what I might become. I don't know when she began, or where, and have no way of knowing if she ever stopped. She's gone from my life, out of sight, but not mind. Maybe she continues her work, creating days as I perceive them, breathing sounds and smells out of dreams, an entire milieu gusted into existence for no purpose but to serve as backdrop for all my interactions, relationships, my entire impact upon this world. Even my death. All of it, contained in Lily's book.

What does that make her? Some deranged, fallen goddess, spinning a story into being then vanishing?

If I can only remember.

I sift through my remaining books, look between and behind the twenty-one ordinary volumes, just in case Lily's book somehow slipped between the others and was momentarily concealed. But nothing's hidden. No salvation.

I take the pile, all twenty-one, out to the dock, all the way to the end. I sit on the edge, dangle my feet into cold green water. At one time, these books seemed like the beginning of something. A new start. Desperate and sad, that's how I was, clinging to any hope.

Flipping through a shelf-worn *Look Homeward, Angel*, I seek any spark of interest. Why did I select these items to keep? None of these words make sense. The language is odd, distant, irrelevant to what I've become. The words are too small. They seek to make up in quantity what they lack in mass. What does any of it matter?

I stop at page seventy-one, trying to exert my will upon the words on the page. Come to life. Speak to me.

Nothing.

I tear out the page, flip it over. Seventy-two, no better. Nothing here but a waste of ink and paper.

I crumple the page, crush it into a tight ball, toss it in the water. The paper floats on the surface as if it weighs nothing. More pages, tear them all. A handful, whole chapters. Once they're loose, I separate each one, crumple every page into its own individual sphere and let it go down the river. The spine cracks, the brittle yellow glue no longer supported by the block of pages. I throw the remainder into the water. The only Thomas Wolfe book I ever owned now floats toward the Pacific Ocean.

There's only one story, a new one. I have no use for a job, a car, friends, an ex-wife.

Leaving the rest of the books on the edge of the dock, I slip inside for my paper shopping bag from *Parfum de Nuit*, and return to sort my candles, incense and matches outside. I burn a cone of incense in my palm, watch it become ash. I lick my thumb and forefinger, pinch the brown ash between them, place it in my mouth. Taste and smell of burned spice, exotic smoke. So insubstantial, I swallow it. Nothing left.

When I'm gone, I'll still be in the book. If I possess a body, it will continue some other place, a different existence. Not solid matter, but intangible. Safer that way. After I lost Michelle, I fell apart. I kept expecting to recover, but never could. With Lily, someone I barely knew, my breakdown was worse. I can't lose someone I never possessed, can't have fallen in love with a stranger. Maybe I was still wounded by Michelle, and managed to superimpose onto Lily all my sad desire for reconciliation. Hunger and need, so pathetically doomed. Lily might have given something, but not what I wanted. I'm the only one who can rescue myself, confront my ghost wife, shed my joyless, sleepless frailty and confusion, and float away. Measurements, durations, the way sizes fail to match, these breakdowns are unimportant. Leave them behind.

I light a match, shield the wind-sputtering flame behind a cupped palm, and hold it to the candle's wick. Inhale the flame, the smoke. Rest the cardamom-scented candle on the cover of a book of Wordsworth poems, place it flat on the surface of the water. A small raft bearing flame. I set it loose.

As the first moves downstream, I light the second candle and pair it with a copy of *Les Fleurs du Mal*. It follows, as if drawn after what went before.

The third candle, the last I own, smokes and sputters from an oily wick. I'm afraid it's too heavy to be supported by the thin paperback of Hemingway's *In Our Time*, but it stands. The river bears it away. Give us peace in our time.

Three candles disappearing.

"Keep." I speak the word. Open another book, write the word on a random page, and set the book loose.

"Hold." I write this in another book. It goes after the one before.

"Stay."

"Wait."

Keep writing, setting loose. So many words, not enough books.

Anyway, I can't stay here. Nothing is left inside. Everything trails off, slips too far away to retrieve. Here or there doesn't matter. Lily said all rivers connect. Every river is the same river.

After midnight, I drive my car. It's been so long, I can't remember the last time.

The graveyard shift crew at Constant Marine is only five men, working close to the water within a lighted, open-walled steel structure. They only return to the main office building at lunchtime, which won't be until four o'clock. Behind that building where I worked for so many years, I find what I need. Nobody below hears or sees. I wheel it to my car, load it in. The hatchback deck gets scraped up, but I don't care. I disappear, driving quiet, headlights dark.

I consider turning on my lights when I hit Marine Drive, decide not to bother.

The wheeled cart of the torch is unwieldy, difficult to get down the ramps to the dock. I take it slow. Though I've never used the torch myself, I've seen it done. It's simple, just a mix of two gases. The acetylene hisses, makes a sharp, identifiable smell until the spark from the igniter catches. The hiss changes, refines. I adjust the mix, add oxygen, turn both knobs until the blue flame sharpens enough to cut. Even in the dark, it's easy.

I lean over the edge to where the first mooring cable connects Karl's house to the dock. The edge of the stranded metal cable heats red, goes orange then yellow. The flame cuts through, molten metal spits. Drops of steel hit the water and steam, while all around, everyone sleeps. Someone might stop me if they recognized what I'm doing. I keep quiet. It's nobody else's business, pertains to no one but myself.

One cable, the next. I step lightly on the dock, careful when I roll the cart between stages. When the last is severed, all that tethers the house to the marina is utility conduit, thicker than the cables. Inside is mostly hollow pipe, water, sewer and electricity. Cutting takes time. I smell a different burn, melting plastic. Flames rise from the conduit, lick the side of the house. Smoke stings my eyes. The fire burns low, rises slowly, so I ignore it, keep cutting. Finally the electric lights inside blink out. When the last pipe gives, water sprays, drenches my face and spews into the river.

Rain falls, transforms the smell of burning. Eventually, rain should stop the fire. The smoke reminds me of Lily.

I leave the cutting rig on the dock and step inside the house. It shifts, cracks. The whole world moves. Water splashes up, as if compressed in a narrowing gap. The house shudders, comes up against the neighboring house, rebounds and scrapes away along the dock. Finally disconnected, floating free, I slip downstream. I know where I'm going, can see what I leave behind, the marina falling away. I stand in the doorway of an empty house, adrift. No connection remains. The first step out, where normally the dock would be, is now open water. Oregon to one side, Washington to the other.

I can't guess how far I might descend this river before some obstacle or dam stops me. If not this river, some other, where the measure of land exposed to sky keeps expanding. I keep promising not to return, but maybe I'll go back some Saturday in June when new grass has grown in to eradicate the black rectangle of mud. Where Lily once lived, I'll walk the perimeter, look for traces of her passage, find none. I'll make my way to the canyon where I caught my first fish. I won't climb down. From above I'll be able to see, through water clear as glass, that no steelhead remain in the pools. It may be passing of time, or changing seasons. Maybe they'll return.

Maybe Lily will be there.

I have to forget all that came before. Too many changes, too fast. Nothing remains but entropy. Broken time.

The fire spreads to all four walls and climbs the roof, casting light across the river. Smoke spins over the water's surface. The heat is almost too much to bear. Raindrops spit into the flames. Upon the night banks of the Columbia, dimly lit orange, are adornments such as I saw on the Kalama before, arrayed in familiar configurations. Though smoke burns my eyes, still I see clearly enough to recognize the hideous displays from the forest near Lily's field and the Kalama's banks.

Not only there. Here as well. So the truth is revealed. I finally understand.

All this is made in my form, designed to resemble me. These dangling structures of bone, leaf and sinew, like mobiles swaying in the wind, gestural artworks of spattered viscera imprinted on canvases of skin, constructs of dead and living parts intermingled in a unified state of decay. Charred fragments, crushed into dirt, to be washed away by rain. The frantic gestures of a doomed man. A life story penned in slashes of blood.

Tangled bits of mortality along a river, all part of me. These are the remains I will become after I burn.

THE END

Michael Griffin's collection, *The Lure of Devouring Light*, was published by Word Horde in 2016, and his novella, *An Ideal Retreat*, came out from Dim Shores at the end of 2016.

His short stories have appeared in magazines like Apex, Black Static, Lovecraft eZine and Strange Aeons, and such anthologies as *The Madness of Dr. Caligari, Autumn Cthulhu*, the Shirley Jackson Award winner, *The Grimscribe's Puppets, The Children of Old Leech* and *Eternal Frankenstein*. Upcoming stories will appear in the Ramsey Campbell tribute, *Darker Companions*, and *Leaves of Necronomicon*.

He's an ambient musician and founder of Hypnos Recordings, an ambient record label he operates with his wife in Portland, Oregon. Michael blogs at griffinwords.com. On Twitter, he posts as @mgsoundvisions.

CPSIA information can be obtained
at www.ICGtesting.com
Printed in the USA
LVOW11s0143170417
530968LV00001B/14/P